TEARS OF AMERICA

TEARS OF AMERICA

Fella

Print information available on the last page.

Rev. date: 06/24/2019

To order additional copies of this book, contact:
Xlibris
1-888-795-4274
www.Xlibris.com
Orders@Xlibris.com
795673

CHAPTER 1

Lexington, South Carolina

Jillian made a left turn into an upscale middle-class suburban neighborhood. Leaning up in his seat, he downed the music that was beating hard through two 12-inch speakers and a 200-watt amp in his off-road Z71 truck. Scaling the neighborhood quietly and not wanting to cause any more attention to himself than necessary, he pulled up to his location—an empty yard which implied an empty house. Hopped out of his truck and walked up to the front door like he belonged there. Retrieving the duplicated key out of his front pants' pocket, he entered the empty home knowing that a young white male wouldn't look suspicious entering an older white female home when she wasn't home.

Inside the house, Jillian took a quick tour of the home, making a mental note of everything he saw of value. His main reason for breaking into the home was a diamond necklace the homeowner wore one night when she and his mother went out to a social gathering. Taking his mother's car leaving him with hers gave him the opportunity to duplicate her key. Taking his time canvassing her abode, he was in no rush. Not only were she and his mother best friends, they were also coworkers, so he knew exactly when she would be coming home.

Making it up the flight of stairs to the master bedroom, Jillian found her jewelry case, opened it, and saw all the gold and the diamonds, and instantly, his reason for burglarizing his mother's best friend's house began to call his name. Instead of taking one necklace, like a true burglar, he emptied the whole case into his pockets. Antsy now ready to be on his, he reasoned with himself. "Alright, alright," he calmed himself. "I might as well clean this bitch out." Recalling all he saw that were of value, "Two 62-inch flex TVs, that laptop, that big-ass change bin. Yeah, I'mma get all that shit."

Retracing his steps in the house, Jillian went to each room where he saw stuff worth value and gathered it all up by the front door, so he could make fast and easy trips to his car and back loading up his newfound goods.

"Nine-one-one operator, what's your emergency?"

Peeking through her living room window, seeing the young white male loading up her neighbor's belongings into his truck bed, Ms. Michelle said into the receiver, after hearing the police operator answer, "Yes, I would like to report a burglary in progress."

"Are you a victim of the burglary?"

"No, it's my neighbor's house being broken into. He's loading all her belongings into his truck," she said frantically.

"Okay, ma'am. What kind of truck is he driving?" the police operator asked, dispatching a patrolman to her residence while getting details.

"A big ol' tan or beige truck, I don't know the name."

"How many people are involved in the burglary?"

"I only see one white guy."

"Can you identify his plate number from where you are?"

"Maybe if I step onto my porch . . ." She headed that way.

"No, Ms. Davis. That will be okay. Your address is 2014 Masters Street?"

"Yes," she said while standing on her porch peering in his direction. "Oh my god, he's taking all her clothes as well."

"A patrolman is already on the way. Please do not engage the suspect."

"He's pulling off. I'm sorry, I wasn't able to get the license plate number. My eyes aren't that good anymore."

"Ms. Davis, what things did you see him load into the vehicle?"

Jogging her memory she said, "A TV, computer, something that looked really heavy to carry, some clothes. I just don't know what's wrong with these kids today, stealing from their own kind." She shook her head in disgrace. "He should be exiting out the neighborhood through Whitehouse Road. That's the only exit out the neighborhood in the direction he's headed."

"Thank you, ma'am. A patrolman should be on his way shortly to retrieve a statement from you."

Jillian finished loading his truck just in time. Pulling off, he spotted the neighbor on her porch peering in his direction while she was on the phone with, who his gut was telling him, was the police. Taking the neighborhood streets 20 mph above the average 10 mph limit, ignoring the speed humps on the road, he turned onto the main highway and blew out a sigh of relief.

Relaxing himself, mind on the scratch he's about to itch, he looked in his rearview and spotted a patrol car coming his way. Sitting up at attention on the steering wheel, weighing his options, the patrolman was a few cars behind him and steadily gaining. As he mashed the gas to put a little distance between them the blue lights came on. "Fuck!" he yelled.

Swerving into the fast lane, cutting the traffic, Jillian did his best to lose the police in the midday rush. Glancing in his rearview, oddly the cop wasn't behind him. Studying the mirror for a second, he spotted the cop. He pulled over an identical Z71 truck to his. He remembered passing by the similar truck when he turned out of the neighborhood; there was only one difference in the vehicles: its occupants were young black guys.

Crossing his heart on chest with two of his fingers then kissing his fingertips, Jillian raised his hand to the roof of his truck, "Thank god for racial profiling." Headed now to the heart of Columbia, South Carolina to pawn his goods Jillian was ready to receive the fruits of his labor.

Walking up on the truck he pulled over onto the side of the road, as traffic crept by, Officer Taft, hand already on the butt of his gun, glared into the cab of the truck looking for visible items of the burglary.

Seeing the officer peering into his truck bed, he felt butterflies forming inside his stomach due to all the badge-on-black violence going on in America. Calvin downed his widow and timidly spoke. "Is everything alright, Officer?"

"I don't know, how about you tell me?" Officer Taft looked into the truck. "You guys out joy riding, smoking a li'l bit weed, coming back there from Whitehouse Road."

"No, sir," said Calvin, "we're coming from school. I'm a senior at Lexington High, and this is my li'l brother." He motioned to his brother in the passenger seat.

"Sure, sure. License and Registration?"

"Yes, sir." Calvin reached for his glove compartment.

"Whoa!" Officer Taft popped the holster to his Glock 40 while he halted him. "Take it easy there, pal," he said clutching the handle to his Glock. "You don't have any weapons in there of any kind, do you?"

Seeing the seriousness in the officer's expression Calvin said, "No, sir" as the officer radioed for backup. "I was just reaching for my license and registration." Deeply afraid of what all the police was capable of because nowadays a traffic stop was equivalent to being a wanted man for murder, especially if you're young and black.

"How about you uncrank the car? Place one hand on the steering wheel and use your other hand to open the glove compartment then back away, so I can make sure you don't have anything in there dangerous you're reaching for." Doing as he was instructed, Officer Taft checked to glove compartment then told the driver to hand over his license and registration.

Handing over his information, Calvin asked, "Can you tell me why I'm being pulled over?"

"When I return," Officer Taft said then walked back to his vehicle to run his name and information.

Looking over to the passenger seat, Calvin told his brother Tyler, "I think you better call Mama and tell her we're being pulled over down the street."

A couple minutes later, Officer Taft returned to the vehicle as soon as backup came and told Calvin, "Everything came back clear. The reason I pulled you was because we got a call stating a couple guys broke into a house in the same kind of car you're driving, and you guys fit the description of the suspects. I'm going to have to ask you to step out the car, so we can search the vehicle."

"Like I told you before, we just came from school, Officer. Maybe you can verify that by calling our school or you will have to wait till my mother comes before you search the car."

"How about go ahead and step out of the vehicle young man?" Officer Taft asked again and tried the door, popping it open.

Looking at the police standing outside his car without the door separating them plus another officer at the passenger door and another approaching to assist the lead officer sent the shivers through Calvin body. "Can we at least wait till my mother shows up?"

"Sir, I'm going to ask you one last time to step out the vehicle," Officer Taft stated in a no-nonsense demeanor.

"She lives . . ." Calvin started but before he could finish Officer Taft struck and was dragging him out of the car by his upper body. Passersbyers were slowing down, watching the traffic stop and some were even recording the scene with their camera phones.

While Calvin was being pulled from the car and placed facedown on the side of the road in handcuffs, the other officer on the passenger side of the car had his gun drawn and was instructing his brother. "Keep your fucking hands up and don't move. Don't fucking move."

Finding nothing in the vehicle related to the burglary, Officer Taft began harassing them. "You guys smoking a little bit of weed," he asked finding a little bit of tobacco on the floor of the car, "where you hide it at? If you make me find it I'mma give you more than a simple ticket since you won't simply tell me where it's at."

"Officer, excuse me, Officer," an older middle-age black woman interrupted the officer's search of the vehicle. "Why are you searching my car without my consent?"

"Ma'am, I assume you are the mother and owner of the vehicle."

"I am," she said highly upset with an ireful attitude.

"We got a call."

"I know all about your call," she cut off Officer Taft off, "saying someone broke into some house. I was on the phone with my youngest son while his brother was being dragged out of the car and I *specifically*," she said with emphasis on specifically, "heard him tell you that you can verify they just left school by calling Lexington High or to wait till I show up to give you consent to search my shit. Now furthermore, after you illegally searched my car, I know you see book bags and school supplies to verify my boy's statement and found not one piece of evidence that they broke into some damn house. So my question is, why are you fuckin' with my kids?"

Officer Taft knew he was in the wrong but still had the power of the badge on his side. "Miss, I ask that you calm down."

"No," she said forcibly, "I'm going to ask you one more time"— mocking his earlier statement to her son—"to release my kids immediately before I get your ID number and press charges on your racist ass."

Coming to the rescue playing both sides was the black officer who helped drag Calvin out the car. "Miss, we're sorry for the inconvenience but your kids just happened to be in the wrong place at the wrong time, matching the description of our suspects, and we had no choice but to search the truck. We found no evidence, so we will be releasing them."

Nodding her head in agreement to what the cop said, the mother told the officer with plenty of sarcasm, "Thank you. And I'm sorry for the inconvenience, but you fit the description of a black man who forgot his skin color and where he came from." She peered at him. "You should be ashamed of yourself. Now get my kids off the damn ground and out those damn handcuffs. They are schoolkids not criminals."

Jillian cleared 700 dollars off two TVs, a laptop, and the change bin he got from his mama's best friend's house. Satisfied with just that for the time being, he made a stop to his friend who kept that bomb-ass meth he loved, spent two hundred with him then he went to another partner who stayed in the hood and kept good crack cocaine and spent two hundred with him. He headed to his final destination, the convenience store where snatched up a case of Steel Reserve 211 and two packs of Camel lights then headed home.

CHAPTER 2

Charleston, South Carolina

"God is good," said the pastor of Graham AME Baptist Church. "All the time," replied the congregation. "And all the time," the pastor continued on with the saying. "God is good," finished the congregation. "Now brothers and sisters, you'll leave here today and have a blessed and beautiful day and remember today's message. If your problems get too heavy for you to carry, just let it go and give it to God. He'll carry it for you. Amen," said the pastor and in unison the congregation replied, "Amen," thus ending the Sunday service.

Outside of the church, sister Eisha and her son Trimpell were greeting church members when Trimpell spotted a dilly friend of their two-party family. "Mama, Mama Kellyn's here."

Looking into the direction her son just mentioned, Eisha easily spotted Kellyn, her friend since junior high, from a crowd of black faces because hers was the only white face in the bunch. It didn't matter to Eisha or Trimpell that Kellyn was a white woman. They both saw her for who she really was, a woman with a good heart. "I thought you weren't going to make it this morning," Eisha said to her while they hugged and she greeted Trimpell with a kiss on the cheek.

"Girl, please, I need me some Jesus in my life. I wasn't going to miss this for nothing in the world."

"Well, good. I hope you feel the same about my Sunday's dinner. I got candy yams, mac and cheese, turkey wings, fried cabbage over white rice, and your favorite tuna salad."

"Eisha," Kellyn said sternly, "you're not supposed to be eating all that greasy food. Girl, did you forget you're a diabetic? And what your doctor said?"

Shrugging her off, "Them doctors told me to do this and they told me to do that. I did it, and now they want to take my arm from me. It's about time I take my problems out of their hands and placed them into the Lord's. He will make sure I'm alright," Eisha said remembering today's message.

How could one dispute the power of God? Hating to accept Eisha's assessment of her situation, but the way she threw God's name around left her with little to no choice but to accept it. Still Kellyn told her, "Well, I'm just going to have to keep you in my prayers, girl." Looking over to Trimpell, she asked, "You wanna ride with me, Trimppy?" and excitedly he said, "Yes, ma'am!"

Getting an early head start for next week's service, Pastor Rue was in his chambers preparing his sermon for next week's message, when he heard a double tap on his door. Hating to be interrupted when God and him were congregating, he threw his pen on his desk and leaned back in his desk chair, folding his hands across his belly. "Come in." The door to his office cracked slowly at first and an unexpected face appeared in the door opening.

"Pastor, is that you?" the man asked.

"Satan, why are you here? This is a place of worship not a place of defilement."

"Oh, Pastor Rue, is this the way to treat guests of God?" the man stepped into the office, still standing in the doorway.

"All God's guest are gone. Service has been over, so I ask you again, Satan why are you here in my chambers interrupting me from doing my godly duties as a pastor and a man of God?"

"Duties." The man stepped into the office, nodding his head, leaving the door ajar behind him, allowing two more unexpected men to enter the office as well. "That's why I'm here. With your duties as a townsman, as a senator, you can contribute so much to our old Charleston."

"Old Charleston," Pastor Rue chuckled at that statement, showing his intimidators he wasn't afraid of whatever they were up to. "My duties is to represent the people who elected me. And Mr. Charley's henchmen," he made sure the guys intimidating him know he knew who they were, "I'm quite sure it wasn't one single person from old Charleston who helped me get where I am at today. So I will continue my duties I have been engrossed in for the people who believe in me. Not help the same people who wouldn't hesitate to skin me then hang me downtown on Rutledge Street, reconstructing old Charleston all over again."

"Aww, Pastor Rue, you're so predictable." The lead henchman walked up to the desk and tossed something wrapped up in a bundle of newspaper on his desk. "My boss told me you would stick with the bill. Needless for me to tell you, there are people who's gonna do everything in their power to see this circus you're trying to create fail at all cost. So my advice to you is save yourself. That's 70,000 dollars, stop the bill. Let us introduce a whole new bill, we advocate it on both sides, we get it passed, you get another 30,000, and we all are happy," he said hands in the air, getting his point across.

"I am a servant of the good Lord Jesus Christ. I will not take no money to hinder my people." Pastor Rue tapped his hands on his chest as he referred to himself and began tapping his index finger on the desk strongly as he spoke. "Blacks are a minority in the country we built from the ground up. We fought for civil rights and equality, and still we are inferior to your kind. We are inferior in your system. Hillary said it best. 'It's a shame when a black man gets pulled for the same thing a white man gets pulled over for, and goes to jail, whereas the white man gets a ticket.' This has got to stop, and the bill I'm advocating for is a start in this area. I will not degrade myself for the likes of you. I will not." He grabbed the bundle of money on his desk and tossed it on the floor at the feet of his intruders. "Take a payoff from the likes of you. Now get out of my office before I have you arrested for bribery."

Smiling, the lead henchman bended over to retrieve the money and spoke, "You're more of a fool than I thought, Pastor." He was shaking his head. "You have no idea what you've just done. Be sure to say your prayers, nigger. You're going to need God and Jesus by the time we're through with you. Maybe even the Holy Spirit." Turning on his heels, he told the menacing-looking men behind him, who were drilling holes through the pastor with their eyes, "Come on, guys. Time to report." Quietly they left the office, leaving Pastor Rue gawking in their wake.

Sitting inside Eisha's small kitchen with both of their stomachs full, while Trimpell played with his PlayStation 4 in the living room, Kellyn and Eisha were in deep conversation. "So when are you scheduled to have your surgery?" Kellyn asked.

"Next week, Wednesday," Eisha said regretfully then changed the subject to something less worrying. "My social security already kicked in, plus my early retirement. So I'll be alright." Thinking about the little amount of money she was going to be receiving, she said tiredly, "If push comes to shoves and times get too hard, I'll just have to get find another job I can work with one arm."

"Work!" Kellyn exclaimed. "That should be the last thing on your mind. Sounds like you should be getting good money."

"I thought I was too. But you know how these systems work. My SS check is 800 dollars a month, and can you believe I slaved my ass off for damn near sixteen years for my job, and they're only giving me partial retirement? Another 800 dollars a month. Together that's barely enough to take care of me and Trimppy, but God will help me find a way," Eisha said, nodding her head. "He always does." She got up from the table, grabbed her and Kellyn's dishes, placed them in the sink, and began to wash them.

Kellyn felt compassion for Eisha. She was a strong, good-natured woman who did the best she could for anybody she could. Yet life took its course, and she caught the bad end of the stick. Had her first child at sixteen, a deadbeat baby daddy left her with the hardship of being a single mother. By the time her son was eighteen, he became a victim of black-on-black violence and left her and Trimppy, who was only seven at the time of his brother's death, to fend for themselves. Poverty, stress, and depression led to disease in her body; and two years later, she was diagnosed as a Type 1 diabetic. A year later, here she was about to receive more government assistance, while already on government assistance, and about to get her arm amputated. Still she was the strongest person Kellyn knew. "Would you like me to watch Trimppy for you while you're in the hospital?" She stood beside Eisha and placed her hand on the arm that wouldn't be there next week.

"No, Kell Bell. I'm going to let my no-good sister keep him for those couple of days. Maybe seeing her nephew would relight that soul of hers and steer her in the right direction."

Kellyn wanted to ask how Camilla, Eisha's sister, was doing, but from the sound of it, the answer was obvious. Still strung out.

"I'm going to need you right by my bedside.'

"And I'll be there."

"Whoa." Eisha's body wobbled like she was off balance. She grabbed the counter to steady herself and placed her hand on her forehead, checking her temperature.

Placing her hand in the small of Eisha's back, Kellyn asked, "Are you okay?"

"I feel a little light-headed, that's all." Eisha began rubbing her temples.

"How about you go on ahead to bed and let me finish up down here and get Trimppy ready for school in the morning."

Loving Kellyn for her heart, Eisha said. "Girl, I just don't know what I'll do without you. You're a lifesaver."

"I wish that were true, Eisha, I wish that were true. Come on, let me get you upstairs," she said while escorting Eisha to her room.

"Alright, class," Miss Romano spoke to her second-grade students. "Does everyone have their flags on their desk ready to be colored?" she asked as she walked up to the chalkboard and pulled down a state map of the USA.

Some students said, "Yes, ma'am," some students were busying themselves with whatever occupied their minds, while others played innocently, ignoring the paper flag on their desk and expecting to be receiving a real flag.

"This ain't no real flag," one student said. "There's not enough stars."

"Look!" pointed another student to the flag that was hanging in the classroom. "That's the flag of America."

"That is the flag of the United States of America, but this is also a flag that has history in our country," Miss Romano said, holding up the piece of paper they were about to be coloring and pointing at the flag. "This is the Confederate flag, the flag that was used by the Southerners in the Civil War."

"Who are the Southerners?" a student asked.

"The Southerners are the states below the Mason-Dixon line. Now can anyone tell me what the Mason-Dixon line is?"

"The line separating the North and the South," a student blurted out.

"Correct. The Southerners are the states south of the Mason-Dixon line."

"You said Civil War . . . well, who were they fighting?" a young boy asked, interested in the thought of war.

"They were at war with the northern states, who called themselves the Union."

"Miss Romano," a female student asked, "why would the South fight North if we are the same country."

"The South wanted to separate themselves from the North, and live by their own rules and beliefs."

"Why do this flag only got not so many stars as the other flag?" the boy said in a child's intriguing improper voice.

"The thirteen stars on the Confederate flag represents the thirteen states in the Confederacy, whereas the fifty stars on the American flag represents the fifty states of the United States of America," Miss Romano said. Questions started to pour in back to back, but the question that caught her attention the most was,

"What did the Confederate flag stand for?"

Ms. Romano dropped the paper flag to her side and thought about a way to answer this question that would not raise more questions. Her mind came up with one word that wasn't hate or racist.

"Freedom," she told her second-grade class. "Freedom for the South to live as they want. Now class, I want everybody to color their flags any color they want, but first we're going to name every one of the Confederate states in each one of the stars. Now looking at the map on the board, who wants to name one of the southern states you think was part of the Confederacy. Who would like to go first?"

Always one to answer questions, Trimpell raised his hand first.

"Yes, Trimpell?"

"South Carolina," he answered.

"Yes, South Carolina is correct. Now South Carolina was the first state to join the Confederacy. So we're going to write South Carolina inside the first star." Miss Romano raised the paper and pointed to the first star.

The school bus pulled up to the bus stop in Ashley Shores apartment complex in North Charleston, South Carolina. Trimpell hopped off the school bus with sixteen other kids from his neighborhood; but unlike other kids, he had to go straight home after school. His mother was more strict on him than other kid's mothers were on them. That was part of Eisha's way of raising him right.

Making it to the front door of his apartment, he tried to push through the door but couldn't. Strangely the door was locked. His mother was usually always home when he came from school. Thinking that maybe she just stepped out for a minute, Trimpell sat there on the porch of his project building and waited patiently for her return.

Watching the neighborhood in motion, kids were playing everywhere. A group of older girls were sitting on the trunk and standing around a parked car. His brother's old friends, the ones his mother called thugs and criminals, were scattered all over the streets. Some were smoking, some were drinking, and some were running up on cars that a blind man can see didn't belong in the hood. The ice cream man was parked in the back of the hood with his music playing on repeat. The main street in the shores was live. Really taking in his neighborhood, Trimpell saw it for what it was, the ghetto!

Suddenly a car skidded off toward the exit, and Trimpell saw his brother's friend come running over to the group of girls standing by the car parked on the side of road. Looking with his eyes and ears, Trimpell could overhear everything that was being said as a couple more dudes ran up to his brother's friend.

"Yo, what happened, my nigga?" a dude with dreads asked.

"That cracker just rode off with my shit, but I managed to snatch the ma fucka wallet he been trying to flex on me with."

"Money been in it?" the guy with the dreads asked.

"Why the fuck you think I snatched it, dummy."

Trimpell saw him check the wallet then heard him yell out, "Who all want ice cream," finding all the money inside the man's wallet. Like flies to a shit pile, the whole hood ran to the ice cream truck.

The sun was out, he was just out of school, and he wanted ice cream too. He got up, ran over, and was the last to get to the ice cream man.

"Li'l Trimppy, what's up? Your mama finally let you out the house," his brother's friend Boysie joked.

"I want some ice cream!" Trimpell demanded.

"Ice cream! Man, you can get some ice cream. Ay, Mr. Simmons give my homeboy little brother whatever ice cream he wants and pack up one of those three-dollar bags of candy for him."

Receiving his goods, he went straight into the firecracker ice cream and heard someone call out his name. Looking back where the voice came from, he saw his neighbor. Making eye contact, the elder woman yelled loud enough for the whole hood to hear, "Boy, get in here!" as if he was caught doing something wrong. He ran to her.

"Boy, what you doing all the way down that street? Your mama knows you down there?"

"No, ma'am," he answered.

"Why your book bag on the porch? Where your mom at?"

Shaking his head and struggling his shoulders, he said, "I don't know. I'm locked out of the house."

"Locked out?" She found that strange also. "Well, get your stuff and come on inside this house till your mama come back. She'll know you're over here."

A couple hours later, once night fell, Shakayna, Trimpell's neighbor's daughter, came bursting into the house, smelling like weed. "Trimppy, you still here?" she said seeing him sitting on the living room floor, watching TV. "Your mama gotta be home, her room light's on."

Hopping up to gather his things quickly because though he was treated like a child of their own where he was, he wanted to be in the confines of his own home. She told him, "Come on, I'm going to take you over there, and let your mama know you been over here."

They walked out the front door and knocked on his. After several attempts, they got no answer. "I'm sure that light hasn't been on. She has to be home. Come on, let's check around back." Walking around back, she asked Trimpell, "You ain't got no house key?"

"No," he said.

"No open windows?"

"No," he replied.

"Well, damn, Trimpell if she don't answer you're going to have to wear one of my new Sunday dresses to school," she joked on him.

Trimpell fired back. "If she didn't answer the front, why knock on the back door?" as they made it to the door.

She thought about it, reached for the door knob, and said, "That's why you shouldn't smoke weed," then she tried it and found it open. She looked at Trimpell and smirked, "The whole time?"

"I didn't know." He threw his hands up.

"Next time, check. Ms. Eisha?" she hollered out, letting her know she was entering her house, and got no response. "At least we can get you some school clothes so you don't have to wear my dresses. Come on."

The house was quiet, too quiet, and too empty that every step up the concrete steps echoed. She spoke just to be speaking as they made their way to his room. "Grab your toothbrush, clean socks, and drawers and—" her words got caught in her throat as she reached the top step. Instinctively, she tried to block Trimpell from seeing what she saw, but it was too late as she heard his small voice say "Mama" upon seeing her lifeless body stretched out on the hallway floor.

Both were frozen in their steps. The only thing moving was the colored Confederate flag Trimpell brought home from school as it dropped from his hands and landed on his mother's chest.

CHAPTER 3

Charleston, South Carolina

"Daddy, when is Mommy coming home?" seven-year-old Christian asked her father as he tucked her into bed for the night, realizing her mother has been missing from her daily duties for almost a week now.

"Soon, Chrissy. Mommy's just taking a vacation. She'll be back soon," Chris told her, ruffling her hair, wishing his words were true. But the truth was, he really didn't know. Their relationship was getting worse and worse by the minute, and her runaways were becoming habitual and always longer than the last one.

"Well, she needs to hurry home, Daddy. I miss her," she whined to her father.

Leaning over and placing a kiss on her forehead, he falsely told her cheerfully, "How about you get comfy in your bed, hold on to Dora," he gave her, her Dora doll, "and y'all both go to sleep with dreams of Mommy and let me go call her and see if I can get her to come home early. Will that work?"

Christian nodded her head, "Yeah."

"Go to sleep, babe, okay?" He wiped a strand of hair from her face like he used to do her mother when problems didn't exist between them.

"Okay, Daddy," she said, and Chris got up to leave her room, digging into his pockets for his cell phone.

"Daddy," she called out to him.

"Yes, sweetie."

"Tell Mommy I love her always and forever."

Chris thought about her last three words, "always and forever," a saying he and her mother used to express their love for each other. He told his daughter, "Sure thing, honey. Now get some rest, school in the morning."

In his room with the door close, Chris called his wife and willed her to answer the phone.

"Yes, Chris," she answered on the seventh ring.

"Again, Carol? Another night you're out running around with niggers and not home with your fucking child."

"Don't you dare put her into this. You know why I'm not there. You know, Chris, and don't you dare involve her into your hate, Chris," Carol said, upset.

"Bitch, your child is here missing you, and you're out running the streets doing drugs with niggers, you whore," Chris silently screamed into the phone, so Christian wouldn't overhear him from the other room. "That's tacky, you bitch. What could those niggers possibly do for you but bring you down."

"No, Chris, you bring me down. That's all you ever did was bring me down. It's you, not them, not my family, my friends but you Chris."

"Me? I'm the one who loves you Carol—me! Not those niggers you're with. They're just using you. I . . . it is I who loves you."

"Love me? How could you love me when all you do is hate? Chris, your hate is what took me away from you. It's what got me where I'm at, in places I thought I would never be again. Your hate is what destroyed us. Keep hating, and it's going to take everything you love away from you. It's going to destroy you like it did me, Chris. What you are is your world."

"Agh, bitch, just bring your ass home," he yelled a little louder trying to hold on to his temper.

She matched his anger. "For what, so you can beat me, so you can rape me? Chris, that's what you want to do, rape me, huh. Black my eyes again. Why, Chris? All I ever did was love you." She cried from all the memories of hurt from the man she loved.

"Just come home, Carol," he begged. "You don't belong with them. You're better than those black niggers you're with."

"No, Chris, no." She was truly sad for him. She knew he was a long way from the change he needed to make in his life. "I don't belong with you. As long as your heart is filled with hate, these black people I'm with will always be better than you."

Hearing his wife say such a thing to him drove him insane. A stream of profanities came pouring from his mouth, revealing pure hate and ignorance from his heart. Silently, she waited till he was done ranting and raving, and when she had the opportunity to speak, she said three words to him before she hung up: "always and forever."

Sitting inside a trap house inside the West Ashley area of Charleston, Carol looked up at her drug-dealer friend, Freeman, who just entered the room where she was staying. Tears rolling down her cheeks, she said to him, "My daughter misses me, but I can't go back there. He's going to end up killing me, if I already ain't dead." She began to cry harder as realization started to set in.

Freeman took a seat beside her and placed his arm around her shoulder, drawing her closer into his embrace. "Damn, sis, I hate to see you like this."

"I know," she said through sniffles.

"Let me ask you a question. Do you love him?" he asked looking her into her eyes.

Returning his gaze, she said, "Always have and always will, but I can't go back. No, not this time. I've got to let him go." She paused and thought about it. "Why you ask?"

"I would've let my li'l niggaz do him for you, free of charge."

Hearing him offering to do such a thing nerved her more than it helped. She knew he only had her best interest at heart. He was a friend of hers since high school, and when Chris's mental and physical abuse drove her back to a life she thought was already behind her, she bumped into Freeman for the first time since school days. It was his heroin she found relief from the pressures in her life. His statement was a further confirmation that she was in a fucked-up situation. But no matter how much Chris accused her of fucking Freeman, how he disrespected her, beat her, molested her, strove to get her to join his clan of hate, she couldn't bring herself to say yeah.

"No," she cried harder. "He got to live to learn. Then he can learn how to live."

"So what you gonna do, C?" he asked using her nickname. "You can't sit up in here and go back down this road. That's not going to help you. You got a little girl, a loving family, stop letting this chump bring you here. Y'all just ain't working. Let that nigga go. I'll come with you, and together we can go get your little girl, and I'll take you to your parents' house."

"Free, it's not that easy."

"The hell if it ain't. You just making excuses. C, look around you. This ain't you. You don't belong here. Enough drugs and guns in here to get you a life sentence. You don't need this shit," he said as he reached for her syringe and dope and threw it as hard as he could at the back of the room door. "Get off this shit, Carol, if not for you, if not for me, then do it for her." He pointed at the picture of Christian on Carol's key chain.

Getting up from where he sat on the bed, Freeman told her, "You're grown. I can't make you do nothing you don't want to do. Nobody can make you do anything you don't want to do. You here 'cause you wanna be. I don't want you to be here. I hate to have to do this to you but be ready in the morning. I'm taking you to go get your daughter or I'll be taking you to his funeral—your choice. And after tomorrow, none of my li'l niggaz serving you no more." And Freeman walked out the room, leaving Carol staring at his back.

Carol felt helpless. She looked on the floor to where her syringe and dope landed, and like a pouncing cat, she pranced off the bed to retrieve it and quickly, she was right back where she sat on the bed with her only hope in the world, that boy. Turning to face the nightstand where her cotton swab, spoon, and lemon juice sat, she went to work getting her a fix ready. Instead of her usual two bags, she wanted to feel nothing, take all the pain away, so she dumped two more bags of heroin into her spoon. Tying herself off around her thigh, liking to hide the vein she shot up in, Carol took her fully loaded fix and felt the heroin pulsing through her veins.

The sound of his cell phone vibrating on the dresser beside his bed woke Chris out of his reverie. "Hello," he answered in a groggy voice. "Yes, this is Chris Cooper. May I ask who's calling?"

"This is Detective Hiers with the Charleston Police Department. I'm deeply sorry and unfortunate to have to tell you this, but I'm here at a residence in the West Ashley area, and there has been a horrible accident."

"Bossman," one of Freeman's trusted capos called him for the second time that evening.

"What's up, Lil Junior, and this better be good."

"Naw, it ain't, bossman. Everything went wrong. We got to pack up and move. This shit is on fire."

"Bitch, get off me." Freeman pushed aside the stripper that was laid buck-naked across his chest and sat up in bed. "What happened, Lil Junior?"

"She OD'd."

CHAPTER 4

Lexington, South Carolina

Two weeks later still on his trip, Jillian was consuming any and every drug he could get his hands on—from meth to crack, cocaine, heroin to prescription pills. Jillian hadn't been home or seen his mother since the night before he broke into her friend's house to support his drug habit. The seven hundred dollars he started out with was gone by the third day of his binge. That's when he started pawning pieces of jewelry to cover his daily fix. The clothes he stole supported him for a day. He found a woman about the same size as his mother's friend and sold her a heap of garments for a Ben Franklin, which got him more meth, more crack, more beer, cigarettes and 3.22 cents worth of gas in his truck.

Pulling up to the closest pharmacy he could find, Jillian was running on fumes. Both his car and himself. He had just pawned his last piece of jewelry and knew the ninety-seven dollars would go farther if he made his own meth and sold enough to re-up and smoke as he pleased. Although he wished he would've came up with the genius plan sooner. Jillian thought, *better late than never*. He walked into the store knowing absolutely nothing about how to make meth, but YouTube showed you step-by-step instructions on how to make ice. That's where he got his list of ingredients from. Getting the minimum amount of material needed to make what he wanted, Jillian spent sixty-one dollars, leaving him with a little over thirty dollars in his pockets. Checking his phone, it was almost two in the afternoon, leaving him with four hours before his mother came home, and plenty of time to turn her house into his meth lab.

"Make sure no moisture is in the air or in the surrounding area," the man on the screen kept saying and Jillian was pretty sure he had that part covered. He moved about the kitchen trying to cook the meth, hide the smell and cleaned up after himself as well. He paid little attention to the perspiration that was building on his body and dripping down his forehead. Leaning over his makeshift meth lab, Jillian heard a small poof right before smoke shot up out of nowhere. Fanning the smoke, trying to get some fresh air as well as a clear view, a blaze of fire revealed itself through the black smoke.

"Oh shit!" Jillian shouted as the kitchen curtain near where he was cooking his meth went ablaze.

Reaching for the glass of water right beside him, quickly thinking, he dashed it on to the raging flame that only grew when the liquid touched it. *Damn,* he thought, remembering that *that* wasn't water at all. He jumped back, smoke burning his throat, causing him to gag and cough. Taking off his shirt and covering his face to block the smoke, he stumbled around accidently bumping into the table causing the other two bottles of meth to fall, further igniting the fire. As the fire reached the floor, it began to burn from the ground up and Jillian had no choice but to run as his makeshift meth lab was turning into a death trap. Jumping through the burning fire to exit the kitchen, Jillian made it just as a loud combustion blasted throughout the house, causing smoke billow out the front door as he made it outside.

Jillian stood shirtless in a daze in his front yard watching the horrific scene play out. He just kept thinking of what he had just done to his mother's house. Jillian was so wrapped up in his own world of thoughts that he was oblivious to his neighbors who were gathering around also watching his mother's home burn down. Minutes later, fire trucks were pulling up, along with the Lexington police.

"Kevin Grant!" Judge Young called out, prompting the young man to rise from his seat and approach the stand. "You're being charged with possession of 5.2 grams of cocaine base with the intent to distribute. Now Mr. Grant, this is your first mark on your record. I see that you have graduated from high school. Let me ask you young man, why the streets instead of college?'

"Your Honor, I have plans to go to college but my family isn't in a stable position and I'm needed to help out."

"Mr. Grant, I've been issuing bonds before you were born and I've heard it all. There's no way you can help your family by getting caught selling 5.2 grams of crack in a school zone. You can help your family by going to college and becoming something of yourself. You don't know me very well and God forbid if you get the chance to, but one thing I can't stand is a smart kid wasting his life away. Is any of your family in court today?" The judge asked, as he glanced around the courtroom.

Kevin looked around before replying, "No sir, Your Honor."

Peering at him over his wire-rimmed glasses, the judge said, "AS they shouldn't be and why would they? Wasting your education on selling drugs. Since you're using your brains for nothing, I'm going to give you something to think about. Your bond is set at seventy-five thousand dollars. Now young man, you have something constructive to do with your mind. Think about how you're going to get out of jail." Judge Young slammed down his gavel and called the next inmate to issue a bond too.

"Next up is," he looked at his court docket, "Jimmie Black." Jimmy stood and came to the bench and immediately Judge Young started on him. "Mr. Black, you have been charged with criminal domestic violence. Is there anything you would like to say to the courts?"

"Ah, yes sir Your Honor," Jimmy stuttered. "Me and my girlfriend were just arguing. We had a little disagreement and misunderstanding that's all. There was no physical contact between us. The officer came and made our situation worse than what it really was." He could tell the judge was really listening to him, so he continued to explain his situation, ending it with what he held as his ace in the hole. "My girlfriend is even in court with me on my behalf."

"Where is she?" The judge asked and immediately she stood. "Young lady, is this true?"

"Yes Your Honor. The officers were totally out of line, almost like they were picking on him and provoking him. I told them he didn't do anything to me and we were just sharing words back and forth. If anything, we should have both been arrested for disorderly conduct."

"I see! young lady you may take a seat." Directing his attention back to Mr. Black, he said, "Here in South Carolina, criminal domestic violence is a serious offense and we do not take it lightly, myself especially. I released a young man without bond on a CDV charge and a week later, he was back in front of me again . . .," he paused, giving more power to his next words, "for murder . . . Mr. Black can you guess who he murdered?"

Jimmy already knew the answer. Everyone in the courtroom that was listening probably did. He just knew now for sure this racist judge was going to slay his black ass for being charged for CDV against, who he knew made matters worse, his Caucasian girlfriend. He lied, "No sir, Your Honor." The judge shook his head.

"Not only did he kill his girlfriend but he also shot her mother, grandmother and her seven-year-old daughter. Luckily, she lived for the sake of humanity because he's through, no matter what. You young people, don't know what love is. You fuss, you fight, you make up, then do it all over again. If you were arrested for CDV, then I believe that's the charge you're guilty of. Therefore, I'm setting your bond at seventy thousand dollars. And don't you worry Mr. Black, if it's true love, she'll come and get you," Judge Young said sarcastically before slamming down his gavel.

"Jillian Booth," Judge Young called up the next person on the docket.

"Yes sir, Your Honor?" Jillian said once he reached the stand.

Looking over his charges, Judge Young said, "Mr. Booth, these are some serious charges you're facing here—manufacturing methamphetamines, miscellaneous damage to a residence . . . Son what were you thinking?"

"I wasn't Your Honor. And I'm truly sorry for having to be in front of you today," Jillian responded, hoping to gain sympathy.

"As you should be Mr. Booth. Whose house did you destroy?"

"My mother's and she's here in court today as well Your Honor," Jillian said as his mother stood with her hands clasped in front of her, hoping the judge caught the sign she was throwing, symbolizing she was an Eastern Star and needed his help for her son.

Judge Young took off his glasses and wiped the imaginary sweat on his forehead with the back of his hand, a gesture indicating she need not to sweat it.

"You're lucky young man to have your mother still stand by you after you've done such a thing. As you've seen, a lot of people are not as lucky as you are and you ought to be ashamed of yourself. Be thankful. I advise you to get your life together young man and stop the bullcrap. I'm going to set your bond at twenty-five thousand dollars. I hope this is an eye opener for you." He slammed his gavel down and slightly nodded his head to Jillian's mother, his sister in Scottish Rite Freemasonry.

"Man fuck that bitch-ass cracker," Kevin spat, pacing the holding cell floor. He was ranting to all the other inmates who had just come back from the bond court along with him. "He gave me that high-ass bond for that little bit of crack!" In anger, he banged his fist into his palm repeatedly as he spoke.

"How much he gave you li'l homie?" an old head asked as he laid on the concrete floor of the holding cell.

"Seventy-five Gs big bruh. I got to sit. My people didn't have enough bread to catch a cab to my bond hearing, so you know they can't come up with no money to post my bond."

"They ain't got no land to put up?" Someone else from the group of men asked.

"Land! My whole family live off the government. We don't own shit. Not even our damn selves. People just locking us up and shit." He mumbled the latter.

"That's the system li'l homie." The old head said. "They give us these high-ass bonds knowing our people can't post these shit which is why we're out here hustling in the first place. It's wicked man. This system is pure wickedness."

"Don't feel bad my nigga," another inmate sitting on the floor of the holding cell with his arms wrapped around his knees lifted his head from resting on top of them said. "That mothafucka slayed me too. Gave me seventy bands for a CDV and me and my old lady wasn't even fighting. Plus she been in court to verify my statement. That racist-ass police should've never locked me up in the first place."

"This is Lexington li'l homie. They all racist round this part of town." The old head spoke and was interrupted by another who shouted out, "Hell yeah! They racist everywhere." Agreeing with the interrupter by nodding his head to his assessment, the old head continued.

"The judges, the police force, the lawyers, the solicitors, the public defenders, the mothafuckas who created this whole system—all racist. It was designed to oppress us not to protect us. That's why you see so much badge-on-black violence going on in the world, they all against us. That's why your bond set at seventy thousand dollars li'l bruh. The system was made to entrap us."

"I feel you my nigga, word I feel you." Another inmate said who was standing with his back against the wall, listening in on the conversation. "They gave this white boy at my job a ticket and he got caught with two ounces of loud. I get caught with four grams I bought to smoke and these mothafuckas locked up my black ass. Bond set at fifty Gs like I robbed a nigga or snatched a bitch purse. Ay, yo, homeboy," he called out to the white boy sitting silently on the bench. "What they got you for?" He asked when he had his attention.

Jillian hated that all the attention was now pointed in his direction. There were seven other white boys in there with him but they pointed him out the bunch. He just knew where this conversation was headed. "I tried to cook up some meth and burned down my mother's house."

"Y'all white boys and that meth. That shit killin' y'all ass out here. What's your bond?" the same guy standing on the wall asked.

"This my first charge so he gave me a twenty-five thousand dollar bond." Jillian said trying to justify the low-bond amount.

"Twenty-five-thousand-dollar bond," Kevin shouted, "your first charge. This my fucking first charge too and your charge is worse than all of our charges. Not only were you manufacturing meth, you burned down a whole fucking house in the process and that racist-ass cracker only gave you twenty-five-thousand-dollar bond. That's fucking crazy," Kevin said mugging Jillian like he wanted to beat him for being white.

"That's the system li'l homie," The old head said. "Kill us," he rubbed his hand down the black skin on his arm and then pointed to Jillian, "and protect them."

"We should beat their fucking ass." Kevin said approaching Jillian who was backing away timidly.

"Naw li'l homie, don't you go putting your hands on them people chern. That's only gonna make your situation worse. You beat them up here." The old head pointed to his mind

Throwing his hands up in defeat while back pedaling away from him Jillian said, "We are not all the same man."

Someone hollered out "Man fuck that. Let that man get his get back on that ma fucker." As kevin continued to size Jillian up, the jam-packed holding cell began to give way to a small arena for the guys to see a quick bout and Kevin threw his guard up.

"Hey back off!" An older white guy jumped up, shoving Jillian out the way.

Two black guys got up, ready to double team the white guy who wanted to play hero. "The fuck you want to do white boy?" One of them said trying to provoke the white man into saying something.

"Hey, what's going on in here?" An officer yelled from out of nowhere then turned back, "I think they are about to start fighting!" and a couple of other officers ran up to the holding cell door to see what was going on.

"Lil' homie I think it's best for you to fall back. You can't win fighting fire with fire. Use your brain, that's what they want you to do," the old head advised Kevin before yelling to the officers, "We alright in here, get y'all fucking ass from by that damn door. Fuck!" Giving them a couple minutes to calm down, the officers left them.

Sitting on the holding cell floor arms still wrapped around his legs, Jimmy Black voiced his opinion. "This shit sad man."

"You right it's sad. It's sad but it's true!" The old head told him then went back to lying down on the holding cell floor, using his shoes as a pillow.

As soon as she found a good bondsman, Jillian's mother posted his bond and waited outside Lexington county jail until he was released from captivity. "Now that you've seen what jail is like, I hope you've had enough of acting up and being around those types of people. The next time you go in there, I'm not coming to get you." She said after he had slid into her car.

"Ma please, I got a super headache and you're making it worse." Jillian pressed his fingertips into his temples. She hadn't stopped preaching to him since he called her to bond him out of jail.

"You got a headache?" she asked taken aback by the ungratefulness of her son. "You just burned my house halfway down. I possibly got to move and go sleep at Shelby's on top of bonding you out of jail, but you have the headache? I should've left you in there with those niggers and thugs since that's what you want to be. Did you hear that judge today? You should be grateful to have someone who cares about your pink behind. Those guys you just left have no one, and you don't appreciate all you have and all I do for you. Jill Jill, you ought to be ashamed of yourself."

Rolling his eyes into the back of his head with his mouth hanging open and his hand on his forehead, Jillian was tired of hearing his mother's mouth. Knowing all she wanted was an apology and some appreciation, he did the best he knew how. "Okay Ma. I'm sorry and thank you, damn! It was a fucking accident!"

"An accident that shouldn't have happened. Now what am I going to tell my friends? My son was cooking meth and burned my house down."

"Tell them you left the stove on or toast in the oven. Ma it's no big deal you've got insurance."

"It's not about my insurance. It's about your behavior."

"Ma, can we talk about something else please? This whole ordeal is irking me."

"Jillian your irking me and you're right for a change. Once we calm down then we'll talk about it, okay?"

"Okay." Jillian agreed but knew the silence wasn't going to last long. She was checking every mirror back to back like she was being followed by someone. He knew it was because she was strung out on Adderall and couldn't sit still or shut up.

"So how was jail?" She asked just to make small talk.

"Ma!" Jillian snapped, aggravated.

"Alright alright. Did you know they just freed that police that was attacked by that massive black guy up in Charlotte, North Carolina?" Jillian only knew what she was talking about because that was another topic in the holding cell he was in.

"I heard Ma and for your information he wasn't attacked. That police officer Derrick shot that school kid in cold blood."

"Hush up Jillian. Don't be around here saying things like that. A black guy walks up on you like he did that officer and you'd shoot him too. These blacks are an intimidating group of people. A violent bunch. They beat up and kill each other . . . imagine what they'll do to you. They just shouldn't be walking up on people like that." Jillian remembered some of the things that were being said about some white people while he was in the presence of young and old black people and he realized a lot of it was true. They were racist, this world was fucked-up. A blind man could see that officer murdered that boy in cold blood and the system set him free saying fuck black lives. Hearing his mother side with the guilty showed him she was racist. But of course he already knew that. He was raised by her, but he himself, was no racist. Fuck white people and black people. He only cared about dead people on colored bills.

"Hey Ma," he said, ignoring her ignorance. "You sleeping at Shelby's?"

"I am. Could you believe someone broke into her home two weeks ago and stole all her belongings? Her neighbor said the thief had a truck the color of yours. You had nothing to do with that right, Jill Jill?"

"Shelby Ma? Come on, you know I wouldn't dare."

"I know Jill Jill, she just told me to ask. Are you coming over? She has plenty of room for us both." Jillian wanted to yell *hell naw* but decided against it.

"Naw I'mma just go over to Reef's. I couldn't imagine a day or more around you and Shelby. Just drop me off to my truck."

"You sure you want to bombard Reef's mom with all those heads over there?"

"I'm sure Mom. I may pop over to Shelby's but I'd rather stay at Reef's. You think I can have about sixty bucks for food and gas, so I won't be freeloading."

"Oh Jillian," she said digging into her purse.

CHAPTER 5

Charleston, South Carolina

Two weeks after Eisha's funeral

While sitting four deep in one of Bridgeview apartment building steps, Skee, Gucci, Junior and Moo Moo were passing blunts back and forth, talking politics.

"Bruh ain't no way Donald Trump beat Hillary Clinton in the presidential election," Junior said. "I was shocked like a mothafucka' when my li'l brother woke me up and told me that. What is the world coming to?" He asked as he grabbed the blunt Moo Moo was handing to him.

"I'm not too surprised she lost," Skee said. "Y'all may think I'm tripping but I read this book called *The Biggest Secret* by David Icke."

"The biggest secret?" Moo Moo mocked, as a cloud of smoke escaped his mouth.

"Yeah man *The Biggest Secret*. The shit implied Hillary and Bill Clinton were coke addicts."

"I can believe it," Gucci said pulling out a big bag full of smaller bags of coke. "This shit runs the world."

"That ain't even the crazy part. The book also said they were aliens, a group of reptiles that secretly run the world." Skee told them feeling like he had their attention.

"Man shut the fuck up Skee," Moo Moo told him. "Y'all niggaz go up that road and start believing in all kinds of shit. Hit this blunt and get your mind right." He passed Moo Moo the blunt of loud. "Blow that for li'l Zavion Dobson."

"Who the hell is Zavion Dobson?" Gucci asked.

"See niggas so worried about coke and don't know who the high school hero is," Moo Moo told him seeing them all looking at him strange. "That's the li'l dude who lost his life saving three girls from gunfire."

"Yeah yeah yeah," Gucci exclaimed. "I heard about that. Let me hit that for li'l Zavion too." He reached for the blunt and Skee jumped back from him.

"Look y'all boy," Junior pointed and they all looked in the direction he gestured to. "Them boy over there fighting!"

"Who them is?" Skee asked dumping ashes on top of Gucci's head.

"That look like big Nessa and the smoker Joe." Moo Moo said getting up from where he sat on the steps and began to walk over to them. "Man fuck that, I'm not going over there." He said turning back around. "They already got the whole damn apartment complex watching them, look at all the li'l kids egging them on. This shit crazy for real man."

"Excuse me," a white woman interjected coming out of nowhere, startling Moo Moo. "Do you guys know where apartment 115 C is at?"

"Police or case worker?" Moo Moo asked. Seeing the woman looking at him, lost by his words he said, "You the police or a case worker?"

"Neither. I'm a friend of Eisha's. I'm looking for her sister Camilla." The strong stench of marijuana the group of young boys was smoking made her want to scrunch her nose but she kept her face straight. It also made her fear for Trimpell. Becoming a product of your environment was real and the last thing she wanted was for him to become another statistic.

"Upstairs, last apt on the left." Junior said, remembering Eisha, Camilla's sister had recently passed away.

She passed the graveyard . . . and her eyes hasn't seen life yet. Only graves. This was no place to raise a child with death so near. Her thoughts were reinforced when she turned into the complex and saw people of all ages running toward two people brawling it out in the middle of the street. Lucky for her, she didn't have to pass the mob. Parking her car around the back of the building, she cautiously walked around to the front and bumped into a group of teenagers no older than Trimpell sitting on the steps of the building, smoking what she knew to be weed. Her earlier assessment was just confirmed: this was no place to raise a child.

Excusing herself and getting the whereabouts to the apartment she was seeking, Kellyn knocked on the door and was confronted with another reinforcement of her previous thoughts. First, it was the stench of stale cigarette smoke. Second, Camilla opened her door wide enough for her to see into her home and she couldn't help but to take notice of three guys sitting in her living room before Camilla obscured her line of sight by placing her body in the door jam.

"May I help you?" Camilla asked with zero tolerance in her tone still holding on to a grudge from years ago.

"Camilla?" Kellyn stated feeling the same energy she always got from Camilla since their falling out. She was over their house while camilla was out and about, chilling in their room since Eisha always had to share a room with her baby sister coming up, she accidentally found some drugs camilla had hid for one of her boyfriends at the same time her mother walked into the room. That got her put out and turned Camilla against her.

"You know I never liked your snooping ass since I met you. How may I help you?" Camilla asked remembering the time they met after she came home from the juvenile detention center. Eisha was already pregnant and kellyn and her were already best friends, close like real sisters, like how she felt Eisha and herself should've been And to make matters worse she blamed Kellyn for getting her kicked out and strung out. If she never left home she would've never fell so hard on drugs.

Caught off guard by Camilla's attitude, Kellyn regained her composure and did what she came to do. "Well, you know that me and Eisha were like this," she crossed her index and middle finger on both hands to demonstrate how close they were. "I tried to speak to you at the funeral but thought better of it. I thought maybe I should give you time to grieve." She nodded her head yeah, as if that was the right decision. "I know it's hard for you already having two kids of your own and maybe taking in Trimppy is only going to add pressure to your problems. Eisha did her best to raise Trimpell right. You know after losing her first child, her dream was to have Trimppy do so much better. I know you want the same for him and I do too. I love him like a son. If it's okay with you, maybe we could work something out on the behalf of his well-being. Maybe we could both take turns in keeping him or I could take full responsibility of him and compensate you in the process." Kellyn suggested full of enthusiasm. "I just want to finish what Eisha started Camilla. I really want the best for him."

"Bitch," Camilla said realizing what she was being asked, "you brought your high and mighty white ass out here to ask me if you can get my sister's son from me, my nephew." Camilla stepped outside on her front porch closing the door behind her and confronting Kellyn offensively.

"No!" Kellyn said, "I'm not trying to take him from you. I just want the best for Trimpell, he deserves it. He's a good child."

"You want the best for him," Camilla scoffed. "Slavery days is over Ms. Kell Bell." She called her by her nickname. "You are not getting my nephew. Yes, times get hard but I'll find a way like I been doing. Now you can take your white ass on and call DSS and report to them all you want 'cause I know that's what you gonna do anyway, like you told on me years ago." Camilla said hand all in Kellyn's face. "That's the problem now with you white people, always sticking your nose in other people's business. Talking 'bout you want to help and all y'all do is hurt people. Fuck!" she spat. "I ain't sharing my nephew with your white ass for you to be all up in my business. Bitch you crazy." Camilla thought for a split second. "Hell, y'all out here killin' y'all own kids, you think I'm just gone hand my nephew over for you to kill too? Wasn't that your cousin who just killed his five kids and stuck them inside a trash can?"

Kellyn was hurt and surprised by the hostility and disrespect she just received from Camilla. All she wanted was to give Trimpell a fighting chance but in doing so, she was insulted and disrespected because of the color of her skin. Camilla had even went as far as asking her if she was related to the white guy who killed his kids and dumped their bodies inside a dumpster. She was speechless.

"Truth hurts doesn't it? If you want to help, let him stay with his own people. That's what he needs. Not you or this racist-ass system to raise him. He needs us, his people," she said backing toward her door.

"You know what Camilla? His people, your people, my people, black people, white people, at the end of the day, we are all people and not all of us are filled with ignorance like yourself." Kellyn stated her peace and took off down the steps, not bothering to excuse herself from the group of teenagers who became onlookers to their exchange of words, leaving Camilla shouting profanities at her back.

As she turned the corner, she heard someone yelling to Camilla, "Your stupid crackhead ass should've let that lady get that damn boy. Dumb bitch she was going to pay you and you could've start paying some of your bills around here."

Then she bumped into Trimpell hopping off the school bus as Camilla yelled back, "Fuck you!" to whoever that was.

"Come here Trimppy," Kellyn said kneeling down and reaching out to him with tears welling up in her eyes.

"What's wrong Kellyn?"

She wanted to tell him everything was wrong but instead thought against it and changed the topic. "Nothing. Here I got you something." She dug into her purse after releasing him from her embrace and placed a cell phone in his hands. "Don't you let anybody get this phone okay? You keep it and you hide it somewhere only you know, okay?" Trimpell nodded his head to her directions. "I got my number saved in there under Kell Bell and I want you to call me anytime you need or want something, you hear me? I don't care if you're hungry, mad, happy or just wanna talk. You just call me okay?"

"Yes ma'am."

"I'm going to be stopping by every so often to check on you. So be expecting me. Here take this." She handed him some money. "You spend that wisely for school lunch and snacks. Okay Trimppy!" He took the money and stuffed it into his pocket.

"Okay." He agreed on the verge of crying himself after seeing the tears fighting to fall down her cheeks.

"You remember all your mommy taught you and stick to it. Just because she's not here doesn't mean you don't have to follow what she told you. You be a good boy Trimppy. Call me and I love you. Come here give me a hug."

"I love you too Kell Bell." He said finding comfort in her embrace.

Walking into his newfound home, Trimpell was called into his aunt's room where she stayed cooped up most of the day. "What that white lady told you?"

"Nothing aunty. She just said how much she loves me and gave me some lunch money for the week." Trimpell replied.

"Lunch money!" She perked up at that "Let me see." She stuck her hand out for the money. Taking the money from his regretful hands, she counted it out. Peeling off five of the thirty-four dollar bills, she gave it to him. "That's five dollars. A dollar for every day of the week next week in school. That should get you a snack every day since you eat free lunch. I'mma hold on to the rest of this money. Now go outside and play." Once Trimpell was gone outside with her two sons, she went into her living room and gave fifteen dollars to one of the dope boys sitting inside her living room, playing Trimpell's PlayStation 4.

"Alright now the house lady need to get something proper for that. Y'all sit y'all ass up in here all damn day. Now it's time to look out."

"Ms. Mary Mack Mack Mack, all dressed in black black black, with silver buttons buttons buttons, all down her dress dress dress." Sang Christian and her friend Zaire as they played pitty pat outside after school while waiting for their parents. So immersed in patting each other hands to the nursery rhyme that Christian didn't see her father pull up.

"Christian, your ride's here!" Her teacher yelled from afar.

"That's my daddy Zai, I've got to go," she said calling her best friend by her nickname. "See you Monday," she said, running off to hop in her father's car as Zaire yelled after her.

"Bye Chrissy."

Hopping into the back seat of her father's car, she leaned forward to hug and kiss him but was stopped in the process.

"Hold on, sit back for a second baby." Chris leaned over reaching his hand into his glove compartment and pulled out his hand sanitizer. One thing he hated was dirty hands but worse than that was a dirty nigger child's hands.

"Give me your hands Chrissy." She reached her hands out and he applied the sanitizer. "Now rub your hands together until they're dry. Honey what have I told you about playing with all kinds of people."

"I know Daddy but Zai's my friend."

"She's not your friend Chrissy. She's black." He told her as he pulled off.

"Yes she is Daddy. We play together every day and she's nice unlike all the other girls in my class."

With complete patience, Chris told her, "Listen Chrissy, white kids shouldn't play with black kids. We're a better people than them. Just a couple years ago, black people couldn't play with white people, could not go to the same schools as white people, couldn't use the same bathroom as white people nor drink out the same fountain as white people," Chris informed her as he merged into the interstate.

"But we do now Daddy. So it's okay for me to play with Zai."

"No Chrissy, it's not. Society wants you to think it is but us as whites have to use our better judgment. Black people and their kids are poor and unhealthy. Black kids should deal with black kids and white kids should deal with white kids."

"I wish I were black so I could play with Zaire." Chris was a racist to his core. His siblings were racist, his parents were racist, their parents were racist, and so on all the way back to their great-great-great-great-grandfather who was the captain of a slave ship. Hearing his daughter say such a thing caused him to swerve in the road and horns to blare out at him.

"Chrissy don't you ever let me hear you say such a thing. You hear me? It was people like Zaire who ran your mommy to her death. Blacks are the scum of the earth and my daughter is too good to play with black kids." He yelled. Calming down he asked, "You love your mommy right?"

Hurt by the sound of his voice, she started to cry.

"Yes sir."

"Well you shouldn't play with those people. She wouldn't want that."

Confused by his words and the way they contradicted with her mother's, Christian thought a moment before responding. "But Mama said you shouldn't judge a person by the color of their skin but by the content of their character. She said everybody was equal and skin don't make the person, it's their heart."

"Chrissy," he said stopping her from going any further. "Mommy was sick remember? Listen darling," Chris lowered his tone a bit, trying to calm her down, "Remember this, we could never be equal with them. We are purer people by nature. God chose us to represent him. Knowing this and understanding who you truly are, you will start to become pure. But for as long as you're running around playing with blacks, you'll be just as dirty as they are."

Later that night, hearing a knock at her door, Camellia grabbed her crack pipe off her dresser top, slipped on her robe around her skinny physique then slipped on her bedroom slippers and made her way through her home. She passed her two sons and nephew playing Trimpell's PS4 in the living room on her way to the front door. Expecting this knock for quite some time, she opened her door already knowing who was on the other side.

"Come on inside to my room," she told him and sashayed her way out of direct sight of the kids. "This still the same stuff?" she asked once they were inside her room. Camilla dug into her robe pocket for the money, letting the robe slip open just in case he wanted something besides money from her.

"Yeah, you got a straight ten dollars."

"If you want the change too," she grabbed the loose change out of her pocket, allowing the robe to open fully exposing herself. "But I got more than that if you want it." He dropped the dime rock on the dresser top and pulled her robe opening farther apart until he was able to take her in from her head to her shaved pussy. Cocking his head to the side, he gave her her answer.

"Maybe later on tonight when the kids asleep. How much you got?"

"Seven dollars but if you coming back go ahead and give me a forty and you don't gotta worry about it later."

"I said maybe."

"Well looking ain't free either, give me a fifteen-cent piece." Camilla begged.

"Just let me get my money," he said shaking his head. "Camilla girl, you're hard to deal with." She handed over her seven dollars, thankful he didn't want the change because it was just enough to get another dime later. "Keep the night open, I might come back for real." Without anything further he turned and left the room. She heard him but was more focused on loading up her crack pipe with the rock she just received. Hearing her front door closed, she glanced up, locking eyes with Trimpell. Shame passed through her soul.

"Ain't I told y'all to go outside and play?" Camilla yelled out of embarrassment rather than for them not following directions.

"But Mama, it's seven o'clock at night."

"I don't give a damn what time it is. The streetlight's on ain't it? So carry y'all ass out there. Y'all ain't gone sit up in here playing that damn game all night. Go!"

Outside behind their apartment building, Trimpell, his older cousin Richie by two years, and his younger cousin Rayquan by a year ran into Kyle, the only white boy their age in the complex.

"Hey y'all come here, look at what I just got," Kyle called out to them.

"That ain't real," Richie said.

"Of course it is. I just got it from Kingston. I got a sale for him," Kyle said, breaking down the weed on the a/c vent.

Looking at the green bud with purple hairs, Trimpell asked, "What's that?"

"Where y'all got this guy from, the suburbs?" Kyle joked. "This is what you call loud. The best of the best weed."

"Weed! You smoke weed?"

"Who doesn't," Kyle asked. "Richie I think your cousin's scared."

"Boy that's my li'l cousin, he ain't scared. Richie told Kyle defending Trimpell.

"Well let's roll up and see. Y'all got a light?" Kyle asked. They all shook their head no and Richie told Rayquan to go get one of their mother's lighters.

"We can't smoke right here, everybody will see us." Kyle looked around nervously then agreed with Richie.

"Come on. I got a spot we can go."

Once Rayquan came back with the lighter, they headed to their duck-off spot and Trimpell was shaking like a falling leaf. Rarely did he ever get the chance to go outside now here he was outside at night about to smoke some weed. His mother would die all over again if she knew what he was doing. Part of him wanted to object, but another part of him wanted to be down.

"Here Trimppy." Rayquan handed him the blunt. "Hit it softly and hold it in and breathe." He took the weed and did as told. He started heaving as the weed entered his virgin lungs.

"Ahhh haaaa." They all started laughing and calling him a newbie.

CHAPTER 6

Lexington, South Carolina

Not even twenty-four hours since his release from county jail, Jillian was back at it. The sixty dollars for food and gas went straight to the meth man and was smoked up in no time. With no more money to get high with, his only source of income was his brain. He had to think of something to get him some money—and fast. Searching the back of his truck bed in his friend Reef's front yard, he was looking for something, anything he could pawn for some money.

"Hey Jill Jill, what ya' looking for?" Reef called out to him, coming out his front door, hearing Jillian pull up. Focused on finding something, Jillian didn't bother answering him. They were friends since forever but Reef's life didn't take the same turn as his. Reef was plain old trailer park trash. All he did was drink bud and fix cars. "If I didn't know any better, I would say you're digging for gold by the way you're digging in that truck bed."

"Shut up Reef." Jillian pulled out a crow bar. "I need some quick cash and you standing there barefoot with that can of beer in your hands telling stupid jokes ain't helping me."

"Quick cash? I swear Jill Jill, you the most money-spending son of a bitch I've ever seen. Ya' might as well take that k-bar there you holding and crack a couple soda machines. It'll get you some quick cash, quick change and quickly get ya more jail time if you get caught. Yo' moms told me you burned down her house, leaving the oven on. Ya might need to slow down some Jill."

"Soda machines . . . how the hell you break into soda machines?" Jillian asked no longer tearing up his truck bed in a hopeless search.

"Take that there bar, jam it in the side where the key goes," he said, motioning with his hands. He pushed the imaginary crowbar he held in his hands in. "Then wala . . . magic."

Sixteen days later, Jillian damn nearly cracked every soda machine in Lexington. He made so much money cracking soda machines at night that he rode around all day, getting high and scoping more soda machines. With his options getting low, he thought maybe it was time to take his show to Columbia, until he found three brand-new soda machines sitting outside a grocery store just begging to be broken. Never one to say no when it was in his favor, Jillian made them his target.

Three machines in one stop, he thought as he moved to the third machine. *I can probably call it quits for the night and take tomorrow off,* he told himself. Just as he was opening the machine, headlights turned on into the parking lot. Automatically he looked to see who it was, but the bright headlights blinded him, causing the crowbar to fall from his hands. Reaching for the crowbar and regaining his sight, he heard screeching brakes, he looked up to find another car coming into the parking lot. *Fuck it's the police,* Jillian thought right before he took off running in the direction of his truck. Rounding the truck, Jillian was blocked from the driver door by the back of one of the officers' police Cruiser, which stopped right beside his truck.

"Hey!" The police yelled, hopping out of his car trying to stop him from fleeing.

Turning on his heels in the other direction, he ran straight into the second police Cruiser head-on. Rolling over the hood, landing on the ground face first and high off meth, he never felt the fall. Instead he struggled to get to his feet and was knocked back down hard by the first officer who pulled up on the scene, when he jumped onto him. "Quit fucking moving!" The officer yelled, trying to pin him down. But Jillian kept fighting. His mind was set on getting away. Seeing the altercation taking place, the second patrolman hopped out of his car and ran to take hold of Jillian's legs.

"Get his arms!" The officer yelled to his partner as he twisted Jillian's legs into a submission move, causing him to give up the struggle.

"Put your fucking hands behind your back!" The initial officer cursed, forcing him to do as he instructed.

"You got him?" Asked the second officer.

"Yeah I got him, he's secure. Either this kid is as mighty as a lion or we're getting old."

"Drugs!" The arresting officer said, lifting Jillian off the ground to place him inside the back of the police car. "Look at him, he's wired." Jillian's eyes were wide, asphalt on his face and in his hair, snot was coming out of his nose and blood and saliva were dripping from his mouth. "Yeah, we're going to have to isolate this guy." Looking at Jillian he asked, "What kind of drugs you on pal?"

Hurt that he was getting arrested and unable to get high again tonight, Jillian let out an aggravated howl.

Conducting a search of his person before they placed him inside the back of the police Cruiser, the arresting officer found the answer to his partners earlier question. Meth!

"Mr. Booth," Judge Young asked Jillian as he stood before him again in bond court. "Weren't you just in front of me a couple weeks ago? If I'm not mistaken, didn't you burn down your mother's home behind the same foolishness you're standing in front of me for, only this time you got a string of strong-armed robberies along with your possession of methamphetamines."

"Yes sir" Jillian responded.

Shaking his head, Judge Young told him, "Rhetorical question son. You have a lot to learn young man and I must say I'm highly disappointed in you. Weeks ago, you had your mother in here standing by your side and today here she is again. You ought to be ashamed of yourself. I did the best I could for you our last meet, but there are procedures I have to follow and you leave me no choice but to revoke your bond."

"Your Honor," his mother called out to the judge, "Is there any alternative? Jail is not the place for my son."

"Ms. Booth, rules are rules. You can hire an attorney, but since your son is out on bond on similar charges and less than a month later he is arrested for the same thing, I have to deny his bond. I'm not sure you understand the extent of what has happened here, so I'll tell you. Lexington police had to set up a small sting operation costing them time, money and manpower. You're right, jail is not the place for someone as young as your son, but he better make the best of it because more than likely, he'll be there until his court date." With that he slammed down his gavel.

Covering her mouth to stifle her cries, Ms. Booth couldn't believe they were taking her son away and locking him away with animals.

"Next up on the dockets is Jabez Beatise."

"Jill Jill," his mother spoke to him through the telephone on the other side of the visitation booth glass. Since his incarceration, visiting him and sending him money became a weekly ritual for her. "I spoke to your lawyer. He's going to push to get you in court soon, so you can get somewhere better. How are they treating you back there?"

"Mom I'm fine. It's these ten years I'm facing that's killing me."

"I know honey. Everybody's doing the best we can for you, me and your lawyer. He says the ten years is what they want to give you, but he's going to get you something less. Nobody has been taking your money right?"

"Mom," he stressed, "stop it okay? I'm fine."

"I'm sorry, I'm sorry. You know us moms worry about these things. I didn't raise you like this or to be around these kinds of people. I don't know what's going on with you back there. Has anybody tried fondling you?"

"Mom," he yelled this time causing her to jump, "this is nothing like you see on TV. People are not getting raped or robbed like jail is portrayed. I'm fine. Nobody's taking my stuff, raping me, beating me up—none of that. And most importantly, most of these people you keep referring to are not like the way you think they are. They are actually good-hearted and cool to hang around with. Maybe you should try it out." Surprised he would suggest something of that nature to her, she widened her eyes and softly shook her head no.

"I'll pass even though me and Shelby ain't talking like we used to." She looked at him shamefully.

"I'm sorry Ma!"

"Jillian, I just don't know what has gotten into you. Of all the things you could've done, why did you do that to Shelby? If it was that bad, I would've given you the money." She cried with tears falling from her eyes.

It turned out that the pieces of jewelry he pawned were insured and when the serial numbers were reported they came back as stolen under his name. Something told him to go to the pawnshop he was known at. Now two weeks after he was arrested, they came with a warrant for his arrest for second-degree burglary on Shelby's house. "I'll write her for you Momma, tell her I'm sorry."

"I would surely appreciate that Jillian." Wiping her eyes she said, "Well visit is almost up. You just keep praying son. Ask God to change you and remember God won't let nothing happen to good people. Okay, I love you and will see you next week."

"I love you too Ma," Jillian said right before she hung up.

Seven months later . . .

Standing in front of the judge in a crowded courtroom alongside his attorney council, Jillian was ready to meet his fate. The judge sat on his podium speaking what Jillian considered the same BS he'd been hearing from his mother and everybody else. No longer threatened with facing ten years, Jillian was ready for whatever they gave him. All his charges were dropped, except the strong-armed robberies on the soda machines. His lawyers got the case for manufacturing, simple possessions, and destruction of property dropped. The letter he wrote to Ms. Shelby turned her heart in his favor and she called the solicitor speaking on his behalf, which, with help from his lawyer, got his second-degree burglary dropped too.

"I hereby sentence you to serve three years inside the department of corrections." The judge finished his touching speech.

Three years didn't sound too appealing until his lawyer explained it couldn't get any sweeter. "You've already got seven months in the county, minus that from the 65 percent of the three years you have to serve, and you're looking at a little over a year. You'll be home before you know it. Plus there's the possibility of parole."

"Jillian it's going to be alright, you hear me," his mother cried. "I already got minutes on the phone and money on your books. Just please stay out of trouble, a year is not long."

"It's not Mom," Jillian said holding on to her as she cried in his arms. He was really headed to prison and fast because the bailiff was already pulling on his arm, pulling him away from his mother.

"Come on son, we've got to go."

At seven the next morning, Jillian along with six other guys were boarding a transportation bus headed to South Carolina's Department of Corrections. Taking a seat by the window, staring out of it in silence, to him everything seemed unreal. People were on the highway going to work, smoking cigarettes, drinking coffee, listening to music; they were actually free and here he was in chains and shackles, unable to enjoy the small things freedom had to offer. He thought about the first time he ever got arrested; how guys were saying whites had it easier than blacks. He wished they could see him now, living proof the system cared about only those who adheres to its inputs and outputs.

Lost in his thoughts the whole bus ride, Jillian's mind came back to him when he saw the sign, Wateree Correctional Institution and the bus pulled to a stop in front of the prison. "Alright fellas." An officer came with a piece of paper in his hand and stood on the bus. "When I call out your name, give me your SCDC number, get off the bus and line up alongside that fence." He began calling out names.

"328238" Jillian called out when his name was called.

"Alright Mr. Booth, go ahead and line up."

Two hours later after the inventory, Jillian had his new living assignment and was on his way to his new ward. Walking down a long tunnel, all he smelled was the stench of nicotine; then it was the musk of thousands of men. He looked to his left and to his right and everything looked like chaos. Wards were on both sides of the tunnel and in each ward, beds were everywhere, people were everywhere, second-hand smoke was everywhere. "WARD 7" the sign read and Jillian knew this was his assigned ward. He stopped in front of the gate and waited for the CO to let him in. A couple steps forward and the gate slammed close behind him. "New meat," someone hollered out and all eyes turned to him and his crew's direction.

"Yo what's up?" A slim guy approached them. "Y'all just coming down." They all shook their heads yeah. "That's what's up, well they call me HB and I got all the weed, all the cigs and k2. If y'all go head and put y'all stuff up, Ms. Graham will let y'all go to the store. Hold up." HB ran to the bars of the ward and hollered out to Ms. Graham. "You gone let the new guys go to the store today."

"HB, get yo ass away from them damn bars, trying to sell that stuff to them guys. Somebody gonna put a stop to you. You watch what I tell you," she hollered back already knowing what he was up to.

"Alright," he replied and turned back to the group of newcomers. "She gon let y'all go. Y'all got money right, well just holler at me."

"How much is cigarettes?" Jillian asked.

"Two dollars a cigarette and they fat too."

"What the hell is k2?"

"You haven't heard about k2?" HB asked, looking at him crazy. "That's the best thing that hit the penitentiary since fuck books."

CHAPTER 7

Nine years old and no longer a house kid, Trimpell was outside running amongst the other kids his age inside the apartment complex, doing anything their young minds come up with. "Let's play nigger knock?" a little boy called Dreadhead suggested as they were walking in the middle of the road.

"I'm tired of ringing bells and running. Half of the doorbells don't work around here anyway. We be running for nothing," Kyle said as he swung a stick at rocks on the ground.

"At least we're getting practice for the police," said Richie. "I saw them catch Skudda last night out the window and they dummied that boy. Slammed him and choked him," he said, imitating the slam and chokehold the police had Skudda in. "He lucky they didn't kill him."

"Maybe we should get some real practice." Trimpell suggested, thinking of all the badge-on-black violence that was going on lately.

Liking the sound of that, Kyle asked, "By doing what?"

"I hid Skudda's gun for him. Maybe it's still there. We could shoot it a couple of times," Dreadhead said, shooting an imaginary gun in the air. "And then the police will come."

Nervous because lately they were getting in too much, Rayquan, the youngest of the bunch said, "Let's just go play black ops. I'm tired of being outside."

"No we got all night to play black ops and if you go into the house, Aunty will be looking for us all. Maybe we could bust a couple windows," Trimpell said, trying to discourage Rayquan from going inside. The house was the last place he wanted to be.

"Ain't nobody got no damn money for y'all to be running around here busting out no damn windows. Bring y'all little bad asses here," Kingston said, overhearing what they were discussing as he passed them in the street. "I got something for y'all lil ass to do."

They all got excited upon hearing that Kingston had something for them to get into. "I got this cracker about to roll through here. I'mma tell him to pull up in that parking lot," he pointed to the parking lot he was referring to. "Now which one of y'all li'l niggaz can count the best?" He asked and Richie pointed to Trimpell. "Trimppy right? You know how to count money?"

Trimpell nodded his head yeah.

"Well I want you to be the one who gets the money. It's supposed to be 1,200 dollars. Get the money and count it before y'all give him anything and when you get it, ask him three times if he is the police while you're counting the money and do it like this, 'You the police?' He should say no. Then ask him again, 'You sure you're not the police?' and when he says no the second time, be like, 'You positive you not the police?' and after he answers no that time, I want each one of y'all to run up and give him one of these." He produced four ounces of weed, handing one to each of them. "Trimppy, make sure you get the money first."

Fifteen minutes later in the apartment building's parking lot, Trimpell stood outside the driver's side window of a Nissan Maxima, asking the driver of the car, a chubby white male "if he was the police." After receiving the money, he began to count it.

"Do I look like the police?" he replied, which wasn't the correct answer. After they got the instructions from Kingston, they had a lot of questions for him, which led him to knowing he was expecting a yes or no answer.

"Wrong answer. Next time, I'm going to run off with the money. Yes or no question, You the police?"

"Hell no, I'm not no fucking cop. I don't know why he sent your ass out here in the first place."

"You sure you're not the police?" Trimpell ignored his disrespect.

"What are you? Deaf, dumb, or stupid? I said no kid."

Trimpell nodded his head to his partners after counting the money and getting the amount he was looking for. They ran up to the car and tossed the weed into it and ran off just as quickly as they appeared, back to where Kingston was hiding in the apartment hallway.

"One thousand two hundred dollars?" He asked as they stopped short of him, breathing hard like they just finished running a marathon.

In between breaths, Trimpell said, "Yeah" handing over the money.

Taking the money and smiling, Kingston said, "You li'l niggas keep it up, and I'm gonna put y'all boys on. Here." He gave Trimpell a gram of weed and a blunt to roll it in. "This a blunt but y'all can make three out of that one, so y'all have to find two more blunts. Use my name if y'all go to the blunt lady. Y'all li'l niggaz stay cool and out of trouble." Kingston gave his salute to them then walked off into the apartment door he was standing by.

Reaching for the weed Kyle said, "Let me roll!" and Trimpell snatched it back away from Kyle.

"Naw it's my turn," he said "I want to roll it."

"You're gonna mess it up newbie," Kyle called him by the nickname they made for him over a year ago when he first started smoking.

"That's why we got three chances." Trimpell said, producing a dollar out of his pocket from the money he got from Kellyn earlier this week.

"Go get the blunts and meet us at the spot." He told Kyle who was always going to get blunts for the dope boys in the hood.

At their smoke spot, sitting on a couple of broken-down a/c vents behind an empty apartment building, Trimpell had his blunt roll and was putting fire to it. Taking a deep breath, barely coughing as he inhaled, he passed it after two more pulls. "That's some gas," he said feeling the weed already. "Take three and pass to Richie, you always hogging up the blunt."

"Shut up newbie. You just started doing this," Richie fired back passing the blunt to Dreadhead after his three hits.

"Let's put two in the air at the same time," said Kyle itching to hit the blunt he just rolled. Out of the five of them, he had the most experience in smoking and rolling. "That way a blunt will always be in rotation."

Appealing to all of their interest Richie said, "Fire up."

Two blunts later and laughing their stomachs to the munchies, Rayquan voiced what they all were feeling. "Man I'm hungry!" And in unison, they all chimed in, "Me too."

"Who got the snacks?" Dreadhead asked.

"Mama doesn't get her EBT till the 16th of the month. What about you Kyle?"

"Man my mom sold it all."

"How about we hit the pantry?" Richie suggested.

Getting up and running to their stash of stolen bikes, Kyle called out, "I got the cruiser."

Leaving Downtown Charleston's aquarium for the afternoon, Chris, spending the day with his daughter, decided on riding through the city to show Chrissy some of their real history, since they were in the area. Cutting through the market he asked, "Do you know why they call this place the market sweetheart?"

In a lovely sweet sing-song voice a nine-year-old girl would have, she answered, "Because this is where they sell things at." She said using her knowledge of what a market was to answer his question.

"That is correct honey, but it also has a deeper meaning. A long time ago our ancestors, my great-great-grandfather and your great-great-great-grandfather would bring slaves from Africa through the middle passage to America and Charleston is where they would dock their boats, come inland, bringing all their slaves, the black people who didn't die on the journey and they would sell them right here at the market. That's why they call this place a market because this is where we used to sell our slaves at baby, not things like they do now. But black people."

Chrissy had no idea what to say of such a horrible thing, so she asked, "My great-great-great-grandfather did these things Daddy?"

Proudly, Chris said, "Yes he sure did baby!" Busting a left on Meeting Street.

"He was a bad man."

"Chrissy you shouldn't say such a thing. Your great-great-great-grandfather was a great man. You should be proud to be related to such a man. Little do you know, it says a lot about who you are, who you come from, the blood that flows through your veins. He's who you got your pretty blue eyes from and your long golden blonde hair." Chris told her. "You see that tree there?" Chris pointed to a huge oak tree in the middle of the road.

"Yes sir." She nodded her head.

"That is the tree we would use when blacks would defy us in any way. We would hang them there in front of a huge crowd of people and in front of other black slaves as well to let them know what would happen if they go against their master words or rebel in any way."

"Daddy if all these bad things happen on the market and at that tree, then why are they still there? Shouldn't they be taken down since these things don't happen no more?"

"Those things don't happen no more but we leave them there as a remembrance for us all Chrissy. A remembrance for who we are and for who they are, the master and the slave. See darling, we gave blacks a chance to prove themselves, to be people, let them get jobs, go to school, learn things but look at what they do. They rob, steal and kill, hurt others. They remained as animals. So instead of going back to the good old days, we now deal with them differently. Lock them away in jails and cages, prisons! So see baby, society may have changed but the heart of it," Chris took his index finger, representing the one percent and tapped it to his chest, saluting his way of life, "is still the same."

Leaving out the city, skipping the interstate and taking Meeting Street extension, the back way to get to Hanahan where they live, Chris wanted Chrissy to see the difference between how she lives and how blacks live. So as they passed the ghetto, project homes, and project kids. Bums after bums walking the streets, hookers. Chris drilled into her how much better she was than black people. "They hate people like us Chrissy, because of what we represent, something they can never be. Pure goodness! People like your great-great-great-grandfather left us with money so we come from something. They have nothing. They never did and they never will." Chris was going on and on till his gas light came on in his Cadillac CTS. "I got to stop and get gas, you want something honey?" Chris asked, pulling into the pantry. "I want a zebra cake," Chrissy said then thought about it. "No I want a brownie, um, how about a lollypop. No Daddy, just get me a Snicker."

"How about you come inside and pick out what you want." Chris told her while parking at the pump. "Come on, let's go inside the store."

Walking into the store, Chris saw the line of customers and said to Chrissy, "Go get what you want honey, while daddy go get our spot in the line. Hurry up!" He said, patting her on the bottom so she can move promptly and Chrissy quickly took off.

Unfamiliar with this store, Chrissy walked down the top of each aisle, looking for the one she was most interested in. Passing the potato chip aisle, she spotted a black and a white youngster, looking like they were up to no good. Her mind ran back to her father words as her eyes took in the candy on the next aisle and she turned into it. "White kids shouldn't play with black kids and as long as you do, you will be just as dirty as they are." kept going through her mind.

"These candy bars are two for 1.50 correct?" A customer asked the cashier at the register, placing two Mr. Goodbars on the countertop. Teissa took the two candy bars and scanned them. For some reason, the discount wasn't showing up on the computer. "Yes sir they are, but it wouldn't read it. I'll just have to type in the discount code." Teissa peered around a line of customers, toward the candy aisle and caught the loveliest little girl walk straight into one of the boys from her apartment complex.

"Oh I'm sorry," Chrissy said, kneeling down to help the little boy she just bumped into, picking up his stuff that dropped from his hands. "I didn't see you standing there."

Having dropped his merchandise out of his hands and loaded with stolen goods, quickly he bent down to retrieve it. "It's OK." He told her, grabbing up some of the Reeses that fell and crouching awkwardly due to a bag of chips that crept down his pants leg.

When the boy squatted down, she heard the rattling of plastic on his body, and by the way he avoided eye contact with her, she knew he was stealing. She could feel his innocence, his embarrassment and not understanding her own feelings at the time, why she was filled with love and compassion for him, she whispered, "You know if you are nervous about doing something, then maybe you shouldn't be doing it." Handing him the candy bars she just picked up off the ground, they made eye contact.

Instantly, her words reminded him of his mother's and looking into her eyes made him think of Kellyn. Thoughts of his life popped into his mind. *I'm nine years old, getting high and stealing out of stores, what am I doing?*

"Here you can have this." She handed him the ten dollars she got from her father earlier today at the aquarium. She wanted to give him so much more after hearing from her father what has been done to him and his people, but the money and her words from her heart was all she had.

Little did she know, that was enough.

Chris stepped up to the cashier and handed her twenty-five for gas. "Pump seven please."

"Would that be all sir?"

Realizing Chrissy was still wandering the store, he glanced around to look for her and spotted her kneeling down alongside some dirty nigger child who just took something from her. Before he could've get her name out of his mouth, he took off for her direction.

Teissa looked strangely at the customer who just took off and went toward the opposite direction, until she saw where he was going, to aid the two kids, one of them being his daughter.

Walking up out of nowhere, startling them both, Chris was filled with rage as he moved past his daughter and shoved the boy. "Get away from her." He spoke as the boy flew hard on to his backside, hitting his head on the concrete floor and crying out in pain.

"Daddy no!" Chrissy cried out, seeing him standing over the crying boy. "It was my fault. I bumped into him."

Ignoring his wailing daughter, using the force of his adulthood, "Give me that." Chris said, snatching the money out of the child's hand seeing when he took it from his daughter.

"He didn't do nothing Daddy." She cried. "I gave it to him."

"Sir?" The manager called out to the customer coming from around the counter. "What's going on sir?" She asked rushing over to them.

Stepping over the heaving boy as four other kids came running up along with the manager, Chris turned to his daughter and said, "No you didn't. And don't you say another word. I saw him take your money. Now get up and come on. Let's go." He grabbed her roughly by the arm and for the first time in her life she snatched away from her father and ran back to the crying boy. "I'm sorry, I didn't mean for this to happen," was all she managed to say before Chris got ahold of her and dragged her out of the store.

Teissa stared at the incident that just transpired in astonishment. *That man just practically assaulted that little boy*, she said to herself loud enough for everyone to hear. Still not believing that was what he just did, hearing the child's cries brought her out of her bewilderment and around the counter to aid the boy.

"Sweetie you OK?" She asked kneeling down beside the child.

"My head, I hit my head," Trimpell cried.

Inspecting the back of his head, she saw no blood but still that boy was wronged and she was now infuriated. "Y'all stay here," she said to him and his friends and got up to go confront the customer who the manager was speaking to outside.

"Sir what's your problem? That's a child, somebody's child. You don't do that to a kid. You need to go and apologize to that damn boy." Teissa said confronting the man and her manager outside at the pump.

"Teissa you need to go back to the store. Customers are in there!" Her manager firmly told her, feeling the tension rising from dealing with an upset customer.

"Really Ms. Lisa?" She asked her manager, a white woman in her midforties. "That man just assaulted that boy and you're worried about customers. That crying child in there, is your customer."

"They were stealing for God's sake." The manager retorted.

"You know what, I'm calling the cops." And Teissa headed back inside the store to her purse for her cell phone. "I'm gonna lock your ass up."

"Fuck off you black bitch."

Ms. Lisa gasped at his choice of words.

"I got your black bitch." She turned around pointing at him with her finger. "Stay your racist ass right there," she said then resumed her stride into the store.

By the time she got her phone, she saw the customer who assaulted the boy starting to pull off and her manager heading back to the store.

"Teissa." She called out to her.

She looked at her like she was crazy to be speaking her name.

"He said the boy assaulted his daughter and took her money."

"That's a damn lie. I sat behind a counter and watched that little girl bump into this boy." She pointed to Trimpell who was standing by the counter, eating a Reese's he was supposed to be stealing. "He was wronged. Customer or not, you do not do that to someone's child. Did you get his plate number?"

"Teissa let it go. The boy is fine. Everything is alright!"

"No, it's not alright. You let that white man get away for assaulting someone's child but the moment one of these black bums or kids come in here stealing beer or candy, you ready to lock they ass up. That's not alright." She shook her head. "I may slave my ass off here for little or nothing but I'll be damned if you treat me the same." Grabbing Trimpell's hand she said, "Come on y'all, get what you came for. I quit." Before she exited the store, she turned back to Ms. Lisa and said, "Now, you got a reason to call the cops."

CHAPTER 8

"Man Hatch," HB stressed quietly to Hatchet, his homeboy from Charleston. "This cracka better have my money." He said as they hid inside the bathroom, smoking a blunt of weed.

"How much he owe you?" Hatchet asked, taking the blunt of weed from him, already knowing who HB was talking about.

"Boy I sting him this week my nigga. I hit him for the whole 100."

"The whole dollar!" Hatchet emphasized softly, then puffed the blunt of weed while shaking his head, wondering why HB credited him that much k2.

Seeing Hatchet's expression, HB said, "Man the cracker been coming through every week since he got here. Some thirty, forty, seventy, fuck it—so far he good money."

"Yeah bruh, but you know how the white boys go. They're liable at any given second to check out." HB agreed with him. "If you gone keep on crediting him, start burning that cracker. Get him out all his people money for a little of nothing. Shit, he gonna buy it and they gone keep on sending it. Slay that ma fucking cracka my nigga. We owe him that you feel me." Hatchet took a hit and blew out the smoke deeply inhaled, "That's how we get our payback." As soon as the words left Hatchet's mouth, Jillian peeked around the wall behind which they were hiding.

"Hb what's up? Come holla at me," Jillian said, sounding cool and hip like he felt he was.

"Alright give me a second. Let me finish this." He showed Jillian the blunt Hatchet just handed him.

"Bet! Everything still good right?" He asked, referring to if he had more k2.

"You already know I'm on deck. I'll be out there in a second." As soon as Jillian walked off, HB looked over to Hatchet and smiled. "He got that bread my nigga." He said whispering, "Yeah he got that bread bruh."

Hatchet returned HB's smile along with a head nod. As long as HB was good, he was too! "Get that money out his pussy ass nigga." HB hit the blunt a couple more times than usual and passed it to him to kill, so he could go and get his money from Jillian before another nigger decided to rob him because of his skin color.

"Jill Jill what's up? You got everything on the list?" HB asked, approaching Jillian who had all the canteen scattered all over his bed.

Grabbing the mash potatoes to show HB, Jillian said. "I took off two honey buns and a pack of cookies to get me a box of mash potatoes, but I got everything else."

"Damn man, you killing me," he cried over the three dollars and thirty-one cents. "Fuck it, you good. Smoking all that k2 is have your li'l ass hungry in it," HB joked.

"Only when I'm not smoking." Jillian laughed then got serious. "Will you let me get a gram now and I owe you twenty-five next week? You know my money's good."

"Damn man Jill. I ain't trying to credit my whole pack to you. Plus you coming with canteen! Honey buns and jack macks ain't gone help pay my mama bills."

"Come on, don't do me like that. I'm good people H, I pay you every week. I'm just trying to smoke and not have to deal with everybody." Jillian stressed while bagging up the canteen, about to hand over his mama's hard-earned money to HB. "What you want an extra ten dollars for it?" HB acted like it wasn't about the money but truthfully that what it was all about. Getting all he could out of this white boy for all white people got out his.

"Man I don't care about no extra ten dollars." He said taking the bag full of groceries.

"Come on H, look out for me." Jillian pleaded. "I fuck with you. I'm not like these other white boys, I'mma pay you your money. I always do."

Like he was doing Jillian a favor, HB said, "Give me a second man, I got you."

"Word man, that's love right there."

Giving him a hard look HB told him, "I want my bread Jillian. Just give me twenty-five." He said knowing he would be back and that's when he planned to hit him across the head with the thirty-five for the gram.

Not even a full two days later, Jillian was in the hole ninety-five with four more days to go in the week and already begging for more dope.

"Naw Jill, you already owe me all your bread next week. I'm not going to give you my shit now and have to wait two whole weeks before I get paid." HB told him, while sitting on his bed watching TV. But that was exactly what he was about to do. Jillian was a gold mine in the penitentiary and HB was digging him dry. A hundred dollars a week was hard to come by and even harder to pass up. He just had to continue to make Jillian think he was doing him a favor and not the other way around. "Anything liable to happen in two weeks. I could get knocked with my phone, lose my pack, go to lock up and you'll just be getting off on me. Two weeks is too risky." He sat up and turned the channel.

"You won't have to wait the whole two weeks, but if push comes to shove you know for sure you will have it then. I'm telling you, I'll find a way to get some more money before then. My mother is going to give me whatever I ask for. It's just the timing" Jillian replied as he squatted down in the space between HB's bunk and his neighbor bunk.

Things were playing out exactly like he wanted. He had Jillian in a hole and he was steadily digging it deeper and deeper. "Man Jill, I don't know man," HB said, really playing him now.

"H I'mma pay you," Jillian said placing a hand on HB's knee. "I promise."

Pushing Jillian's hand off his leg, HB said in a threatening manner. "Look, I'mma do this shit for you." He jabbed a finger in Jillian's face inches away from hitting him for the intimidation tactic. "I'm go ahead and give you 100 dollars' worth of dope now, so you don't got to bother me till you got my fucking money. And you better have my fucking money. Word Jillian, I don't want to have to fuck you up."

Elated Jillian said, "Have I never not pay you your money? I got you."

It took Jillian two days and all that k2 to realize he was being played. HB came to him first with sweet deals, giving him the dope till store day. When he saw that was working, gradually the deals ceased, and their roles switched. He became the one asking for a credit deal till store day. Next the grams got smaller and smaller while the price jumped from twenty-five to thirty-five. Now it was the threats and nasty attitudes. *They must think I'm blind to the game they're running*, Jillian thought as he left out the ward and headed for breakfast.

"Get inside the yellow line." Major James hollered to everyone inside the hallway of the tunnel. "You," she pointed out, "must be deaf or got a problem. I said get inside the yellow line."

"Actually I do got a problem."

Looking at him like he was crazy, she said, "Oh you got a problem, what kind of problem you got? Rolling up on me like that inside my tunnel."

Waiting till everyone passed them in the hallway, Jillian said, "I can't go back in that ward."

"And why is that?" She asked suspiciously.

"They keep taking my stuff." He said half truthfully.

"And who is they?"

"Everybody, first they stole my lock and was stealing my food. Now they just taking it."

"No sir, you got to be more specific than that. You in Ward 7, right? Today y'all store day, who you owe?"

"Nobody."

"Let me see your hands."

"My hands?"

"Yes, your hands. Just like this." She opened her hands palms up and he did the same. "Yeah, you smoking. Stupid why y'all don't wash the residue off y'all hands at least. And ya wonder why prison so pack, ya tell on y'all self." She showed her competence. "Now who you owe and can't pay or I'mma send your ass right back in there."

He didn't expect checking out would be so hard and going back into that ward was not an option. "Major James, you know how it is. I tell you who, you go and confront them and there would be no place on this yard where I could sleep at. How about I tell you the spot he hide his phone at."

"Come on, let's go in my office," Major James said and led the way to her office.

Jillian gave up more than a phone and a name to the Major in order to check in. He told on the whole rundown inside his old ward—all that were hustling, who smoked, who had cell phones. He gave more than he intended to, just to be thrown inside lock up for two days and placed inside another ward.

Lucky for him his new ward store day was tomorrow and his mother just sent his money the day before.

Itching to get high since the morning he checked in, Jillian scoped out the scene to see who had all the k2 and as always the black guy with the most going on. New in the ward and couldn't get nothing on his face, Jillian found himself a conspirator. Another white dude who at first glance you could tell get high by his rugged appearance and on top of that, he was the light man. The guy everybody went to for a light. "You think he'll give me something till tomorrow. I'll pay for it," Jillian asked.

"He knows I don't have any money. You got a better chance going to him yourself."

"Well how about you go and give him a heads up. I got plenty money."

"Man Kenya's cool. He'll do it." Then White Bread thought about it. "You gone smoke with me if I go and do it?" He asked not wanting to hook him up with Kenya and not smoke.

"You got the light right?" When White Bread said yeah, Jillian told him, "Well you know I'mma smoke with you. Go talk to him," he urged him.

The three bags he got for ten dollars took Jillian through the night and had him first in line to go to the store the next morning. He had it all planned out. Pay the ten dollars he owed, buy two grams for fifty dollars and hold on to the other forty dollars to buy more k2 later on. What he didn't think of till he was out in the hallway leading the line to the canteen was that the canteen was right in front of Ward 7, his old ward—HB's ward.

Passing the ward while headed to the canteen, Jillian stole a peek inside the ward and majority of the ward was asleep.

Sliding his canteen list through the hole in the window and moving up to the bagging up area, Jillian got his bags ready to load his groceries when he heard someone holler out, "White boy!" By the sound of the voice, he knew it wasn't HB, and knew they were calling out to him.

Looking back, he saw Hatchet.

"You got that money fuck boy?"

He said the first thing that came to mind. "How y'all supposed to get it?"

"That ain't no problem just pass that shit through these bars." Hatchet stopped someone and whispered to them.

Jillian kept on bagging up his groceries as Hatchet yelled to the guy he whispered to, "Hurry up."

"What ward you should in?'

"Six," Jillian told him nervously.

"What you buck on the major for dummy. That been some stupid ass shit. A check-out move if you ask me." Nothing was new in the penitentiary. The move he pulled, they've seen it a thousand times before on store day. Do some dumb shit, go to lock up so you don't have to pay your bill.

"I was geeking." Jillian told him. The bagger finished bagging up the groceries and he grabbed a hold of his bags as Hatchet instructed him on how to pass the bag inside the ward. He walked toward the bars where Hatchet stood reaching for the bag and tightened his grip on the bag and handed it toward Hatchet. "Oh shit that's the Major," Jillian said knowing passing groceries off was a no no.

Quickly, he shot pass Hatchet.

Glancing into the ward, he saw the guy Hatchet whispered to, talking to HB and pointing in his direction.

As Hatchet screamed profanities in his wake, HB began to yell. "Look here!" hopping out his bed.

Picking up his pace while Hatchet continued to try to stop him and ignoring HB, Jillian made his getaway and heard HB holler, "Don't you worry cracker. I'mma get my fucking bread out your police ass." Knowing Jillian had something to do with the police running up in the ward that night he went to jail.

At the same time, Major James came strolling into the hallway for real this time overhearing HB also. She made eye contact with Jillian and took off in the other direction. "Only one police around here and that's me. Now who owes who and how?" Jillian heard her say as he kept going to his ward.

Later on that night, as soon as the ward lights were off, Jillian and White Bread sparked up a blunt of k2. By the time Jillian touched it, passed it to White Bread and the blunt made it back to him, he was so high, his whole perception of things changed. The air got denser, the smell became stronger, the sight his eyes took in became more vivid, and his thoughts went from worriless to paranoia.

Something wasn't right—he could feel it.

"Here take the blunt." White Bread kept trying to pass him the blunt.

Jillian looked at him strangely then it hitted him. He realized White Bread wasn't right either.

"Man don't start tripping dude, take the blunt."

Jillian focused on White Bread trying to get him to hit the blunt and he voiced his thoughts aloud, so high, not knowing he was even speaking. "You trying to set me up?"

"Set you up! Yeah dude, you tripping. Maybe you really don't need to hit this blunt." White Bread said pulling the blunt back and taking him a hard pull, ignoring Jillian.

Jillian sat there on his bunk and he couldn't shake off the feeling that something was up. Yeah, he was high, but for some reason, something was telling him that White Bread knew exactly what was going on.

He looked around and it seemed everybody was looking his direction, even White Bread who was still offering him the blunt.

Suddenly someone came and dropped down on the foot of his bed, causing him to jump. "Your name Jillian right?" The dude asked.

"Yeah." He answered timidly.

"My people told me you checked in with his change. I," he pointed at himself, "got to get that from you. Now where it's at?"

"Your people?" He tried playing ignorant to what was going on. "Who is your people?"

"Come on white boy. We don't gotta go through this. You owe my homeboy 200, now open up that fucking locker." Snuggle said aggressively and went to open the locker.

"Hold on," Jillian stopped him. "I got his money." Jillian said squeezing on to his locker key he had hidden out of sight in his hand. "I have to call my mother to get it." He said feeling like now was the perfect time for him to call her. "You can come with me in the phone room to verify it. Man I got his money."

Following Jillian into the phone room and standing next to him as he dialed the number, Snuggle listened to his conversation when he conversed with his mother. "Mom, I'm in deep shit," he paused. "No no no, nothing like that. I accidentally broke someone's TV and now I have to pay for it." He listened to what she was saying. "It was an accident Mom." She had to be questioning him. "Yes, if I don't pay for it. I'm probably going to have to fight the guy."

He was good, Snuggle thought.

"It's 200 bucks. No don't send it to my card. He needs a PayPal card." He paused again. "Mom, please stop asking so much questions." He started listening again. "From a drug store or go to Walmart. Mom, I really don't want to get into it with this guy. Tonight will be best." He placed the phone by Snuggle's ear so he could hear his mother's voice and Snuggle nodded to him so he could finish doing what he was doing. "Well I'm going to call back tonight and if I can't, I'll call back in the morning. Okay thanks Mom." He hung up the phone. "I'mma try calling her back in an hour but guarantee I'll have it in the morning."

For the next two hours, Jillian was in and out of the phone room calling his mother. Seeing this, Snuggle rolled on him while he was at his bed and asked him intimidatingly, "You ain't get that money yet?" Stuttering Jillian said, "She's not back yet. I don't know what's going on. But I'll have it by the morning."

"Man you better get that bread bruh." Snuggle told him. "I suppose to punish your fucking ass but I'm not gonna beat you. I'mma spare you. Just get that bread white boy, word!" Snuggle left him sitting there on his bed to go and holler at Meek in the phone room.

"Man if that cracka give me that 200 dollars, him and HB dead. I'mma take that and power up."

"You ain't get it yet?" Meek asked looking crazy at Snuggle.

"He said he ain't get it yet."

"Man bruh that cracka lying. I been sitting right here talking to my old lady when he write the numbers down. Dumb ass cracka even called them shit back out to her. If I had a pen or been thinking I would write it down or had my old lady copy that number and I would've shit all y'all out that 200."

"Word my nigger," Snuggle asked feeling played.

"I been sitting right here." Meek took the phone and pressed it against his shoulder and whispered, "I put that on boss bruh that white boy been got them numbers."

"I bout to beat his ass for playing with me."

Snuggle walked straight out the phone room, headed to Jillian and as if knowing he was coming to him, Jillian was coming his way. "I'm going to try her" was all he got to say before Snuggle wrapped his fat hand around Jillian's boney throat and choked slammed him onto the bed and concrete floor.

"Where the fuck you put those numbers at. You trying to play me cracker boy." He chopped him upside his head.

"I told you she didn't answer." Jillian said between breaths as he tried his best to guard his face from the punches Snuggle was slowly but strongly landing on him.

"Quit fucking lying. I'll beat your ass to death in here."

"Hey hey hey, what's going on in here?" The officer on posts asked, coming to stand at the bar with his flashlight, hearing all the commotion. "Y'all want me to turn these lights on."

Inmates started to scream obscenities at the officers to get him through, but the only voice he heard was the one that sounded helpless and was the loudest out them all.

"CO, help! CO, help!" Jillian yelled over and over again.

Snuggle swung at him with all his might, landing a clean shot to his jaw, shutting him up for a second. But Jillian was right back at it and Snuggle hopped up off him at the same time all the lights came on in the ward and the intercom buzz. "First responders to Ward 6, second response, stand by."

Down in Ward 7, hearing the first response being called to Ward 6, HB told Hatchet as they were punishing food from having the munchies, "I hope they kill that cracker, my nigger."

As soon as Major James got to work the next morning, she found out at briefing what happened to Jillian. Since he was one of her snitches and she knew she could trust him to crash again, place himself in a situation where he would have to tell again. She did the best she could for him by assigning him to a dorm disconnected from the happenings inside the tunnel. Plus this was where majority of the contraband on the yard was coming from and she needed more eyes and ears here than any place else. Under this guise of helping him, with two other officers, one on each side of her for the illusion of power, she strode into the holding cell where he was currently held up until further notice. "Mr. Booth, I'm not gonna lock your ass up this time," she said very directly.

"But I didn't."

"Apt be quite," she cut him off. "There's a million reasons why I can have you placed in lock up, but I'm not." Pointing her index finger at him now, "Whatever you're doing, you better stop it. I promise you the next time your name comes up on my yard," she jabbed herself in the chest when she referred to herself, then pointed back to him when she referred to him, "I'mma going to lock your ass up inside a one-man cell, script your bony white tail naked and keep you in there till you ween off that shit." She said, exasperated. "I know this behind that damn k2. What is wrong with y'all round here? Don't you know people are dying from smoking that shit." She told him sincerely, "Stop it, you hear me. It ain't good for you. Now I'mma place you back there in Dorm 3 away from the tunnel so whatever you got going on in the tunnel, stays in the tunnel. Don't go back there with the same shit. Them boys hop on you, ain't gone be too much help for you. And you better take heed. So that's your one and only warning. An officer will be by to escort you there in a couple minutes." Major James turned on her heels and left out as quickly as she came in.

Dorm 3 was totally different from the wards in the tunnel. It was way less chaotic and more orderly. The inmates seemed more civilized and the living area was cubicles, which provided a little bit more privacy. And for four wings of the dorm there was only one officer. Major James was right, wasn't too much help if he did get into something. But that wasn't part of his plan. All he wanted to do was get high and dorm three was the place to be if you wanted to smoke or buy anything because everything was cheaper and plentiful.

Lucky for him, that ass cutting he took along with his black eye got him exactly where he needed to be. In Dorm 3 with his 200-dollar PayPal, Jillian wasted no time finding information on the best deal he could get with what he had.

"1.5 gram pouches of k2 for fifty dollars, 3 grand pouches for 100 dollars and 10 gram pouches for 200 dollars." His informer told him as they smoked a cigarette in the bathroom.

"Well who I gotta holla at?" Jillian asked and was pointed into the direction of a big black dude with a mouthful of gold from Charleston named Teddy.

Knowing a 200-dollar PayPal card spoke for itself, Jillian approached Teddy and told him what he was seeking.

"Goddamn boy, who the fuck you be fighting? Rocky Balboa," Teddy said, jumping back from the sight of his black eye. "You ain't steal that PayPal from somebody, ain't it? I ain't trying to get my card jam up."

"No somebody tried to take it for me. I got it from my mom. That first response last night in Ward 6," Teddy acted skeptical already hearing of what transpired between his homeboys and a white dude. "Yeah, that was me. I'm good people. Those guys were just trying to get over on me. You know how it is though, take advantage of the white boy."

"Yeah, I know how it is. You know I got to check it first, and if it's good, I will get it to you in about ten or fifteen minutes." Sensing Teddy was a good guy, "Sure," Jillian said, "it's good." And he handed it over.

Thirty minutes later, given Teddy ample amount of time to check his dot and get him his pack, Jillian was ready to smoke like he wanted, however he wanted and when he wanted. From what he was told, a ten-gram pouch of k2 was equivalent to about thirty penitentiary grams. Hearing that, all his patience were thrown out the window.

Looking for Teddy, he found him in the back of the dorm smoking a cigarette with a couple of dudes who were all looking at him strangely when he stepped forward. "Everything worked out smoothly?" He asked.

Teddy made an aggressive step forward and told him, "You dead. I ain't giving you shit. You done shit on my homeboys, who the fuck I look like. Eat that and get on through."

"So you just do me like that?" Jillian asked surprisingly. "Take my money and not give me nothing?"

"Nigga we let your pussy ass stay in here. We can black your other eye, send your bitch ass up out here, so be thankful, bitch boy and get on through before I let my old school right here rip that ass of yours open." Teddy tapped Shango on the arm, who stared at him like he wanted to kill him then fuck him.

"I love white meat. I ain't had a good piece of chicken in thirty-two years."

Realizing that with those massive arms, Shango could literally take him and however he wanted, Jillian wasted no time high-tailing his ass away from them. Remembering the Major's earlier words, "Ain't too much help back there."

With a black eye, no food to eat, no dope to smoke, no nothing at all, Jillian was feeling hopeless. Telling a couple guys what happened, he found out his name and situation was everywhere on the yard and everybody knew he ran off with HB's money. He even found out he had two grams and a fifty dollar pay pal on his head, after receiving his first lesson inside the penitentiary: "You can't run, you can't hide, so just pay your debt and keep on doing what you doing."

Now his face was fucked up two ways, nobody was going to sell him anything since the Charleston boys had all the work and literally, it was over with for him. He had to start anew and he had only one way to do it. He checked the time on the clock saw that it was after 8:00 p.m. and he went to the phone room. Hearing her say "Hello," Jillian said, "Mom, you gotta get me off this yard."

"Ten minutes to 9:00 p.m. standing roll call count," the announcer came on over the loudspeaker and before she can finish her announcement, seven officers bursted into the dorm. "Everybody get by your beds right now. Line up!"

Inmates started to scatter like roaches. They had phones out, some were smoking, some were trying to run and stash stuff. Someone even dropped the phone and walked off, knowing usually seven officers before count meant a massive shakedown.

"Look what I got," Lieutenant Abraham said, kneeling down to retrieve the phone lying there. "Someone dropped their phone." She said, waving it in the air, knowing that no one was going to claim it. "We didn't even come here for contraband and you giving it away. Well thank you." She said, walking down the aisle along with the other six officers.

"You," Lieutenant Benjamin said, approaching Jillian and tossing him a green bag. "Pack up all your stuff, Momma's boy. You going to lock up."

CHAPTER 9

Charleston, South Carolina

"Come on Chrissy. It's bedtime. You got school in the morning." Chris told his daughter as he came into the living room. He had just finished doing the dishes and he turned the TV off upon hearing his daughter watching shows he forbid in his home for no other reason than black people were the stars on the show.

He was anti-black to the core. His mother and father, their parents and their parents were, so should his daughter be. Chris was bound to make sure of that. She just had so much of her mother in her and not enough of him. But practice makes perfect and he could see she was coming along.

"But Daddy," Chrissy whined, "it's early."

"You could've stayed out later if only you were mindful of what you were watching. So that's your punishment."

Pouting with her bottom lip poking out she said, "I'm sorry Daddy. I won't watch it no more." Remembering the beating she got for disrespecting her father at the gas station.

"You better not. Now go run yourself a bath and get ready for bed."

"Yes sir," she said while dragging her Dora doll along with her toward the back of the house.

Chris knew the only way to break her from socializing with blacks was through strong discipline and punishment every time she stepped out of line. So he wasn't cutting her no slack. He knew more about black people than they knew about themselves. That's why he didn't want her watching their TV shows or listening to their music. They are a very alluring group of people and indirectly interacting with them will incline her to take interest and involvement in them. He's even planning on placing her into another school, a predominantly white school, limiting her choice of friendship and who she socializes with. He's refusing to let what happened to her mother, happen to her.

In the living room while watching a blank screen, Chris heard the water start running and he knew Chrissy was getting into the tub. With nothing else to do for the night, Chris dozed off, allowing his mind to take him down memory lane.

"Come on, let's go show Mommy." He told his daughter once he had her dressed in her Halloween costume. Walking into the bedroom where Carol was getting herself ready for the Halloween party they were attending, Chris happily said, "Surprise!"—showing off what he thought was a good costume for a child.

Disapproving in what she saw the instant she laid eyes on the mask that covered her three-year-old daughter's face, Carol went berserk berating Chris's incompetence. "What is wrong with you Chris? Take that thing off her face," she said, slightly screaming while running up to her child and snatching the clansman mask off her child. "Why would you even think of dressing up our child as a clansman? That is so stupid. Do you know what people would think about us?" She asked with a distasteful face.

"To hell what people think. That's their problem now. They don't think enough."

"No Chris, you don't think enough. You're still living in the past. This is 2017 not the '70s. You really need to change your thoughts Chris," Carol told him with sympathy in her voice and heart for him, "because nothing good is ever going to come to you thinking like you do. Change honey." She caressed his face. "Now please go take that robe off my baby and put on her Easter dress. She's going to be a loving princess for Halloween," Carol kissed Chrissy on the cheek, "and hurry up Chris, before we be late."

Chris stirred in his sleep, rolled over and another dream flooded his mind.

Bursting into his front door in a rush, due to running late for his march one morning, Chris saw Carol and Chrissy sitting there on the couch in the living room, lounging, still in their bedclothes. "Why aren't you guys ready?" He asked as he remembered telling her to be ready by 10:00 a.m.

"Really Chris? You know how I feel about that and you expect me to join in your festivities, ah no. I have black friends who I love. I'm not going. I wouldn't risk being seen at a KKK march—me or my child."

"Carol, I thought we already discussed this. You and Chrissy are coming to the march for no other reason than to support me. Everybody else's wife and kids are going to be there and so should mine. Now please get up and get you both dressed and ready to go. I'm already running late."

"We did discuss this and I thought about it. If I support you by going there, then I'm supporting the whole movement, the whole reason why you guys are out there in robes and mask and I don't support that Chris. Everybody's wife and kids are going to be there because they are racist pricks. I am not a racist and neither is my child and you shouldn't be either. A black man or woman hasn't done a damn thing to you or for you. Yet you're out there condemning them in the dark. Martin Luther King said, 'You're all a bunch of cowards hiding behind a mask.'"

Smack! Chris slapped her hard, causing her to hold her face and cry.

"Don't you ever quote a word that nigger said to me out of your mouth bitch. Ever!" He hollered, causing Carol to jump back in fear on the couch and clutched Chrissy tighter. "Get your ass up and get ready."

Terrified, Carol told him through tears, "I'd rather you beat me and miss the march, than I go and get dressed to go with you."

The images in his mind of her holding on to their child faded and he heard her voice. "Hate is an energy Chris. It attracts what you hate into your life."

His deceased wife's words caused him to stir again in his sleep. Relaxing a bit, Chris went straight back to sleep and another memory filled his mind.

Chris pulled into his yard and was surprised to see Carol's car home early as well as another car. He thought, *Some surprises just weren't meant to be.*

Walking into his home he heard voices in the kitchen and overheard his wife say, "Oh shit, that's Chris." He knew something wasn't right by the tone of her voice. Carol shot out of the kitchen with a huge smile on her face before he reached where she was.

"Baby, I want you to meet my friend Janet from work. She is helping me pick out some things for our coming baby." She patted her stomach then said, "And be nice Chris." Trying to soften him up for the rude awakening he was about to get as they walked into the kitchen.

"Hi Chris." Jane stuck out her small black manicured hand, introducing herself to Chris and he just left it there.

Carol looked and saw the indifferent look on his face and wished they had chosen to kick it at the restaurant instead of her home. She just wasn't up to it when Janet suggested it. She wanted her home, now she wished she wanted differently.

Chris looked at Janet's hand hung in midair, heard her say how she heard so much about him and couldn't believe Carol allowed this hooker in his home. "Oh you have," Chris said. "Well you should know I don't want you in my house. So please, get the fuck out." He said in an even voice with no emotion.

Janet stood there in shock for two seconds, till she finally grasped what happened. She couldn't find her keys fast enough as Carol was sincerely apologizing. "You know what Carol, save it. I should have known better when I saw that racist-ass Confederate flag flying outside your door. I'm gone." She turned to leave Carol's house.

"No Janet, don't go. I'm so sorry," Carol cried leaving the house behind her.

"Let her leave." Chris said to her, reaching for her arm, trying to pull her back.

"Get off me," she screamed. "Get your fucking hands off me. Don't touch me Chris." She made it outside, running after Janet. "Janet forgive me. I am so sorry this happened." She told her, ignoring the cramps she was feeling in her stomach.

"Carol, quit chasing that black nigger bitch and get your ass back in here." Chris came and stood in their doorway.

"Shut up Chris," she yelled back. "I'm so sick and tired of this shit with you. I never hated nobody in my life but I hate you. You're disrespectful. This is my friend Chris," she cried.

"Are you going to let me leave or I need to call the cops for you to move your car," Janet asked Chris standing at her car door, ignoring Carol's apologies.

"I should let your monkey ass push it out of the way black bitch," Chris mumbled, going into his pocket for keys. "Here," he tossed the keys at Carol, "let that nigger lover move it for you."

"Ahhhh," Carol screamed, tired of his disrespect; she hefted up a huge rock off the ground and tried to toss it at Chris.

"Carol stop girl, you're pregnant," Janet hollered seeing her exert herself but Carol was in full motion and when she released the stone from her hands, so did her bloody bowels release from between her legs. "Oh my gosh, I'm calling the police." Janet said running to aid Carol, who also just threw her baby out of her mouth.

Chris drifted off into blackness; no more visions of his memories replayed in his mind, but only Carol last words to him lingered: "Your hate is what took me away from you. Your hate is what destroyed us. Keep hating Chris and it's going to take everything you love from you. Always and forever."

Boom, his front door came flying off its hinges.

Rousing from his sleep, he took in three gunmen entering his home.

The first intruder shot over in his direction and whipped him with the pistol upside his head. "Where the fuck is Legend? Where the fuck is Legend?" He asked repeatedly.

"I don't know who you're talking about!" Chris yelled, blocking blows from his attacker.

"Where the fuck is he?"

"I don't know!" He kept telling the intruder. "I don't know him. You got the wrong house. You got the wrong house!" He repeatedly told him.

"Y'all niggaz search the fucking house." The intruder on top of Chris told his partners.

Unable to go to sleep, Chrissy heard all the commotion going on out front and she hopped out of bed to see what was going on. Walking into the hallway, she saw a silhouette run into the kitchen. "Daddy?" She said at the same time the other gunmen turned into the hallway.

Jumping back from the sight of the little girl, a single gunshot went off.

Hearing his name called right before the shot sounded off, Chris's eyes got as wide as golf balls as he stared at his daughter's chest, where a huge hole formed.

Simultaneously, one of the gunman came running out of the kitchen with his gun out ready to blaze fire.

"She scared the shit out of me. I didn't know it was just a child." The murderer said, looking over his shoulder at the little girl.

The gunman who came out of the kitchen said, "We got the fucking wrong house. Man come on, let's go." and tugged on the murderer. "Come on man, come on." And the three jack boys ran out of the house.

Chris began to breathe irregularly as he stared at his daughter's body lying there unmoving on the hallway floor. *Hate is an energy that attracts you to what you hate*, kept replaying in his mind as he crawled near to his daughter's body. "Chrissy, it's okay baby. They're gone. Get up baby. Everything's going to be all right. Come on baby, get up."

Your hate is going to destroy you, Chris. As he got near to her body, a crimson red stain began to appear on her shirt, getting bigger by the second as blood poured out from the wound in her chest. *Your hate is going to take everything you love from you.*

"I'm sorry baby. Daddy's so sorry. Please baby, get up. I am so, so sorry. Please baby, get up." He began to cry realizing she was gone. "I didn't believe . . . God, I didn't believe. Noooo!" Chris cried out in pain, staring at his daughter, who he was holding on to with most of her chest missing.

"You stupid ass nigger," said the murderer's big homie, who had him beaten and tied up in a chair inside an abandoned trailer. "You risked the lives of your homies on a bullshitting ass lick, then you scary ass shoot a fucking child. Nigga you know the fucking heat your no-good dumbass just brought down on the whole fucking city. Cops already killing us for traffic stops, now it's about to be open season on niggers."

"It was the wrong house bruh. He was turning in when we were leaving out. Him and the neighbor had the same car." He gave his excuse for his fuckup.

"Nigga shut up." He pistol whipped him one more time. "You fucked up, that's all. We don't get no room for fuckups in this blood life bruh. Ay Lil Spazz?"

"What it is big home." One of his li'l niggas answered.

"Get rid of this fuckup for me." The murderer began to squeal and squirm.

"I ain't got no problem with that." Spazz cocked back the .40-caliber pistol and placed one in the chamber. He walked straight up in front of his one-time homie and raised the gun dead center to his forehead, while his homie began to scream, with no hesitation, "Blah!" he domed checked him.

"Now that's a fucking slug," their big homie said. "Let's roll."

The Band Perry played in the background of Chrissy's funeral. *If I die young . . . Bury me in satin . . . Lay me down on a bed of roses . . . Sink me in the river at dawn . . . Send me away with the words of a love song . . .*

Chrissy was getting laid to rest in a white coffin covered with white roses.

The murder of a nine-year-old white female by masked gunmen who entered the wrong house was a slap on the face of the Cooper family's legacy and the news of the incident swept across the city, bringing out many old-town conservatives to her funeral.

The city's top politicians came to show their respects and gave their condolences. The chief of police, the Klan came dressed up in suits and ties, family members and friends of the family—all came to give their condolences and respect.

To an ordinary passerby, it would seem all the white people of Charleston was at her funeral and today was a sad day for them all.

Chrissy was a symbol of love as well as every other young female child. As the last bit of dirt was being thrown into her grave on her casket, God began to weep and tears fell from heaven.

Chris's brother Tommy, who was a cop from the North Charleston Police Department, approached him as he sat in the first seat of the front row, oblivious to the rain that hid the tears that rolled down his cheeks as he stared at his daughter's final resting place.

Shielding him from the rain with an umbrella and taking the seat next to him he said, "I love you bro. Just stay strong. This battle isn't over. There's casualty in every fight, but the war is still raging. It's up to you if she dies in vain. The power of God is on your side, use it. We're suiting up tonight. I know you're probably not up to it, but you know where we're at," he told him, asking if Chris wanted to seek some immediate vengeance on a race of people. "Come on, the limos waiting on us."

CHAPTER 10

"Mom," Jillian said into the phone receiver. "Mom, can you hear me?"

"Jill Jill I'm so happy to hear from you. I was worried sick. What took you so long to call me and check in?" Stopping in the middle of rinsing her rice off, she said as soon as she heard his voice on the other end.

"They locked me up at Wateree in protective custody till they were able to ship me. I'm at Allendale now."

"I know, I know," she said happy to be talking to her son and knowing he was fine. "I called headquarters and told them everything you told me. I did a little bit of enquiring, talked to the right person who assured me they will do the best they could for you. You know good people look out for good people." She interjected in her own sentence. Turning her voice down, she whispered into the phone as if what she was about to say wouldn't be heard. "They say that place you're at, is the best yard in the system. Even has a program that guarantees parole." She started back rinsing her rice off.

"Yeah I'm in that dorm. My roommate told me all about it."

"Oh you've got a roommate. Who is he? Is he good people?" She asked, placing the rice on the stove.

"He is white. Majority of this dorm is white." Jillian looked around inside the phone booth to see if any of the other three occupants overheard him. Though the dorm was majority white, black guys were still there and the last thing he wanted was to be considered a racist.

"Well that's good. Y'all probably won't be having too much trouble going on in there then. So what's he like. Is he young? Old? Has he done a lot of time? Is he gay?"

Not surprised she would ask such a question, his mother was just being herself. He said, "No Mom. Well," he corrected himself, cause truthfully he didn't know; it's hard to tell with these guys, if they were suspect or not, "I hope he's not. He seems cool. He's a young guy, a couple years older than me. We really haven't got a chance to feel each other out yet. Since I came he's been with his friends all day."

"Is his friends good people?"

"Mom," he said agitated, tired of hearing her refer to all white people as good people.

"I'm just asking. No need to get all irritated. Sounds like they're some good ole boys. You need to find you some good company." Jillian laughed to himself at her suggestion. That was the first thing he did when he got inside the door after unpacking. "And stay out of trouble."

"I have Mom, that's why I'm calling now. We don't go to the store till next week Wednesday and today is Wednesday. So this whole week I have to go without food. They fed me nothing on PC."

"Nothing?" She asked.

Realizing that she misunderstood his use of the word "nothing," he told her, "Yeah, they fed me but the food wasn't nothing. I need you to go to that store and get me one of those forty-dollar PayPal cards."

"That card I got you the last time."

"Yes Mom, that card. So I can buy some food from this good guy who's going to look out for me." Using her terminology for persuasion.

"Well give me about twenty minutes. I got me some rice cooking and I'll go and get it.

"Thanks Mom."

"OK, just call back in twenty minutes."

An hour later, Jillian had him a fat gram of k2 and was in his room, sitting at the desk, rolling a blunt of it up when his roommate walked in. "You smoke B-blue?" Jillian asked him.

"Nah, I'm a health nut. I don't smoke, I don't drink and you shouldn't either. It's bad for you," B-blue said taking off his shirt and tossing it on his bed.

"But it feels good when you get high." Jillian laughed at his own joke.

"I bet." Looking over Jillian's shoulder, B-blue said, "That looks like k2." Shaking his head, he said, "If I did smoke, that surely wouldn't be it. Is that a gram? Who you got that from?" He asked, looking at the size of Jillian's purchase and knew who ever sold it to, him got off on him.

"That guy Mice." He told him.

"You should fuck with my brother Country. He will look out for you, since you're his own kind."

"Own kind?" Jillian asked with a contorted face, not comprehending what he meant by that.

Looking back at him as if he was a fool, B-blue said. "Own kind, skin color, white." Thinking... *Damn this guy is green.*

"Oh!" Jillian said with a double meaning. Now he understood what *own kind* meant and secondly, *oh you're one of those good boys.* "Well maybe next time. This space rocket is about to take off." He said as he finished rolling the blunt and twirling it around in the air, finding the blunt a resting spot in his mouth.

"All I'm going to tell you brother, is don't crash. Especially fucking with the wrong kind. When you're in a place like this, all you got is your own kind. Welcome to Allendale."

A couple of weeks later, B-blue walked into his brother Airi's room with his hands full of food, where Airi, Country and Job waited on him to bring his share of their store-day meal. Sliding past Airi, who was preparing their food on top of his locker and spreading Job and Country apart, who was sitting on Airi's bed, joking and playing around as usual,

B-blue dropped a can of corn, a can of mushroom, a pack of jack mac, and two soups onto Airi's bed. "Y'all sitting here rushing me to get my shit and you two don't have your shares yet." He said, looking at what Airi was preparing.

"We wage a bet with this turd," Country said to B-blue. "Now he has to put up our share." He high-fived Job who was still laughing at Airi.

"Dude," B-blue said to Airi, "you let these two sucker you into betting one of their stupid bets."

"They're stupid," replied Airi, laughing at the stupidity of the bet he made. "How about you jack asses laugh and bet your way to the microwave before someone else gets there before us. You know its store day and everybody's going to be trying to cook. Here," he handed Country the bowl of sausages, "put this in the microwave. I bet you can't cook that without burning it."

"Bet." Country stuck out his fist. "Call it and you got it."

"See, I told you they were stupid," Airi said to B-blue, leaving Country's fist in the air, knowing better to bet on something stupid like that.

B-blue shook his head and smiled as Country retorted back at Airi and Job, got off the bed and went to the door to peep out the window since Airi mentioned someone else getting the microwave before them.

Job looked and saw Mice going to one of the microwaves. "If we want to cook, we better hurry up because that fucking coon just got a microwave. Only one more left."

Still tripping, Country ran out of the room screaming, "Nigger alert, nigger alert!" with the bowl of sausages in his hand.

Gathered around the microwave as Airi whipped up their food, no more jokes were being said amongst them. Everyone had straight faces on, along with their uniform and ID. This is how they carried themselves out in public, not that they were trying to be other than themselves—they just lived by a code of conduct. Fun and games were cool when it was just them but always when out in public, they represented the one percent of the world population. The supreme.

Posted with his arms across his mid-torso and with his back on the wall observing his surroundings, next to the table where the microwave sat, Country leaned forward and whispered to B-blue, "What's up with your roommate?" He saw him shoot across the dorm with two big bags of grocery, going in the opposite direction of his room.

Finding his roommate using Country's eyesight direction, B-blue knew exactly what was up with him. "He's a nigger lover that's what's up. Every week he's giving up all his or shall I say his mother's money to a fucking coon. Watch him." He told Country and sure enough, Jillian walked straight up to Mice at the microwave and handed him over 100-cold-cash-dollars' worth of grocery.

Mice smiled as the food was given to him in front of everybody on the rock. "Your roommate is a stupid cracker. Feeding a fucking horse."

Over hearing what B-blue and Country were talking about, Job, the highest rank of them asked, "You got to tighten up on him, Blonde and Blue. Are you preaching to him?"

"Every night," B-blue answered. "But he's so lost mentally. He can only see what he wants. He can't fathom things being more than what they appear to be. He sees me as a racist." Still with his eyes on his roommate and Mice who looked like he was in the process of giving Jillian more k2.

"Are you a racist?" Job asked.

"What?" B-blue exclaimed, caught off guard as Country and Airi listened on.

"Are you one who believes that a race or shall I say your race is superior to others?" Job repeated the question a little bit slower and differently for B-blue, his baby brother.

Not having to think about it as he saw Mice slid Jillian the k2, "Yeah if you put it that way," B- blue said and watched Jillian turn to walk off and looked in their direction.

"There is no other way to put it but that way. So if you are a racist and he sees you as a racist, show him why you are racist and why he sees you as one, so he can see for himself. And know," Job said with emphasis on each word using his fingers, "that there's always more than what there appears to be." He finished right before Jillian made his way to them.

"What's up?" He approached with his hands up to dap Job, like he was cool to hip.

Job looked at him in the face, like the devil was trying to tempt him again and turned his back on Jillian.

Feeling played and stupid, Jillian said with both his hands up now, "It's like that? I'm just trying to speak to you man." Job ignored him and started conversing with Airi, who was still at the microwave cooking. "That's messed up dude," Jillian said and walked off, not bothering to speak to anyone else in that hate group, wondering why everyone else did, even blacks.

Lockdown came around 7:00 p.m. at night, right before shift change. Jillian was in his room smoked-out high, out of his mind, while B-blue was in there punishing his bowl of food after a hardcore workout. "That food sure smells good. What you got in there?"

Before he answered him, B-blue just looked at him like, *Yeah, you are really lost. You just gave all his food away to some nigga who don't give a fuck about you, don't have a bite to eat, or better yet a bar soap to wash yo ass, and is about to ask for some of my food.*

"Jack mack." He told him coldly.

Jillian must have missed the hint because his next words were, "Let me taste some." And stuck out his dirty hands.

B-blue thought of what Job told him earlier and said, "You know what, I shouldn't give you shit. But I want to show you something. In the penitentiary, where people rob, steal, kill, and even fuck for food, an easy way to get someone to listen to you, especially someone with nothing, is to feed them."

B-blue got up, grabbed a small cereal bowl, and filled it with rice, corn mushroom, chunks of sausages, soups, and jack mack then handed the bowl to Jillian, who sat up out his bed and started devouring it. "Now tomorrow, go ask that nigga Mice when you see him cooking up all that food you brought him, to give you some of his food. See if he gives you a spoonful or better yet, holla at him when you see him smoking. Ask if you can get a hit of his cigarette or blunt. You'll more than likely get a finger burn or his black ass would probably give it to the ground before he give it to you and watch you pick it up off the ground then tell you, 'Oh my bad, I forgot,'" B-blue said sitting his bowl down on the desk and stood up to look at Jillian. "And keep in mind, this is the same nigga, you," he pointed at him and got louder as he went on, "giving all your mama's hard-earned money to. The same nigga who's giving you them small ass grams. Here," he bent over and dug into his sock, "look at this." He tossed Jillian one of Country's grams he was going to sell for him in the morning. "That's two of those little ass grams that coon's giving you." Tapping his chest with power, B-blue said, "That's why I am who I am. I'm all for my own people because I know," he tapped himself again in the chest, "other people don't give a fuck about me, you, your mama, or my fucking mama. They don't give a fuck about nobody with my pure skin. With my blonde hair," he said rubbing on the little bit of hair visible on his head, "and my blue eyes. That's why I'm racist. If you want to know why Job turned his back on you, that's why. He knows what I know, and we know what you're failing to see. Niggers don't give a fuck about you. You better open your eyes, brother. The nigger you're feeding won't spit on you if you were burning. He wouldn't give you water in hell. And that's who you want acceptance from? That's who you turning your back on your own kind for? Then you got the nerve to wonder why your own kind, the chosen people, turn their backs on you."

Jillian sat there astounded, listening to his roommate go off for him aggressively.

Calming down, B-blue said, "You need to learn your history bro. And quit running around here, smoking all that damn chemical. It's altering your sight. You can't even see clearly. Not through here"—he pointed at his eyes—"but through here," he said, jabbing his index finger at his forehead. "You about to go home, get another chance at freedom and some people will never see that again. We wish we had the opportunity you got and you're wasting it, chasing niggers. Read the Old Testament Jillian. He brought us out of the land of Egypt, the land of the blacks . . . why are you running back? Look at what he did every time we forsake him." He spoke softly. "He punished us. Can't you see he's punishing you. You came here with a black eye. I'm willing to bet you anything you got, that came from a nigger."

Jillian dropped his head at the truth of B-blue words.

Backing up and taking a seat on his bunk, B-blue said, "I ask you to do one thing whenever you see that nigger eating or smoking, ask him. And see what he'd do for you, then remember what I did for you and what you do for him and what you ever did for me. Just ask." Picking up his bowl from when he sat it on the desk and lying down on his bunk, B-blue said, "then you will see why I'm a racist."

Two days later and down and out on his luck, Jillian was broke, with no money, no food and no k2. He was back where he hated to be and always when he ended up, on fumes. It was midday Sunday afternoon and everyone was either in their room, in the day room watching football, or in the showers getting high. With his credit limit ran up to the max, he was unable to get any k2. He figured since he smoked with just about everybody who asked him to hit his blunt, he should be able to get a couple of hits from the guys in the shower room.

Stepping into the smoke area, people were in all corners of the shower, fully clothed and blowing big sticks of everything they had to smoke. Looking for nobody in particular, just anybody he could bum a hit or two from, he spotted Mice and Fat Boy over in the back corner of the bathroom and knew he could get a hit or two from Mice, since he spent all his money on him. He made his way to where they were at. "Yo, Mice let me hit that one time?"

Fat Boy started to laugh as Mice looked at Jillian crazy.

"Come on man, all the business we do? All I want to do is hit it one time."

"Never mix business with pleasure," Mice replied. "This personal here, my nigga," he told Jillian. "Me and Fat got no plans on passing this."

Jillian couldn't believe Mice just handled him like that. Then suddenly B-blue's words popped into his mind. Not wanting to believe he was being played by more niggers, Jillian stooped even lower. "Well let me get the roach?" Jillian asked Mice and saw the light man, Shot Out step up.

"Back off that, white boy, I done called for that roach," the old school told him and Fat Boy began to laugh harder.

"Yeah man, I already told Shot Out he can get it."

Jillian wanted to let Mice have it so bad, but he knew he had no place with these niggers. Out of curiosity he asked, "Well damn, let me get a bag of chips. I'm hungry as fuck."

"What the fuck I look like, a fucking charity? Man please get the fuck from around me with that begging and shit. I'm trying to get high, my nigga," Mice said to him and moved over a couple steps so Jillian won't be in his face any longer.

B-blue was right and he had no choice but to admit it. In one month, he spent 440 dollars with Mice and the sorry bastard won't even let him touch his blunt nor give him a 50-cent bag of potato chips.

Leaving the shower with his head hung low, the last thing on Jillian's mind was getting high. He wanted payback. Not just on Mice but on every nigger who ever played him.

With nowhere to go, Jillian went inside the dayroom and he looked around and what he saw was segregation in 3D. There were about thirty people in the dayroom, eight of them were black, three of them were old and they sat together in the front bench where all the old folks sat, with a little space, clearly, a stay–on–your–side–of–the–bench space, between them, sat the older white guys. The five other black young guys weren't even sitting on the benches. They were huddled in a corner of the dayroom watching TV in their own little world. He thought back to all his interactions with blacks and recalled all the forced smiles and false affection. They weren't his kind. And oddly it seemed to him, his whole life, people were trying to show him that. Staring at the TV absentmindedly the news headline caught his attention. He read the caption, unable to hear the TV because he didn't have a radio to tune into the station. "Man killed on Charleston's market." Then the dead man's picture popped up. Today became a rude awakening for him as he stared at the familiar face on TV. Not wanting to believe his own eyes, he ran to the phone room.

"Mom," he said when she answered. "Did you see the news?"

"Yes baby I saw it. I just got off the phone with his mom."

"No Mom, say it ain't so."

"Yes Lord, it is so. They killed Reef for little of nothing. Three black guys tried to rob him and ended up killing him. The police got two of them in custody now. They're still looking for the third nigger now. I hope the police lock them bastards away till they die and the devil burn them in hell."

Talking to his mother about what happened for the remainder of the call, Jillian walked into his room with a new revelation, looking like he walked through hell to get it.

Seeing him, B-blue asked, "Are you alright?"

Plopping down on the desk, Jillian said, "You were right. That nigger wouldn't give me a fifty-cent bag of chips or a roach. Then to top it off, three niggers just robbed and killed my best friend. Guess what they got off him, fifty-two dollars. They took his life for fifty-two dollars. Stupid niggers."

CHAPTER 11

Charleston, South Carolina

"All squad cars, possible sighting of a wanted person. Considered armed and dangerous. Murder suspect in the Bridgeview Apartment Complex, Building 115." Ran through the dispatcher to all police CB in the local area.

"Yes Kell Bell I'm staying out of trouble." Trimpell said on the cell phone he was holding up to his ear. He was standing in his apartment building hallway, talking to Kellyn, knowing if she heard all the commotion going on inside Camilla's house that she will either pop up or have too many questions. Thinking fast to the question "Why he missed school three times this week?" He answered falsely instead of telling the truth, that he and his cousins were cutting school to work for Kingston. "I missed the school bus and Aunt Camilla doesn't have a car." As she continued to question him, he fired off answers. "I overslept. Around ten. I hate history class." He told her hoping that explained the reasons for his low grades.

Slowly walking down the steps while Kelly scolded him till he reached the bottom step and sat there, Trimpell said sadly, "I miss my mommy." Kellyn sounded so much like her as she berated him for his unkempt behavior. He could sense Kellyn's whole attitude change as she cooed awww and her voice became affectionate.

"Things were different when she was here." He said as tears started to form in his eyes. He loved his aunt and cousins but he missed the love of his mother. That wake up in the morning "I love you Mama" love, even when times were hard, that feel-good love. Now living with his aunt, the only love around beside the love he had for them, was that hard love. That get-it-how-you-live love. That eat-or-get-eaten love, that street love.

Feeling solemn and wanting a taste of the love that used to be so fulfilling, plentiful and abundant, Trimpell asked Kellyn—as three police cars shot by and he absentmindedly reached for the piece of blunt in his pocket, which he stole from the guy in his aunt's house—"Can I come with you?"

Boom boom boom! Nana heard the knocking at her door and she knew it was the police even before the officer said, "Charleston PD."

That was quick, she thought as she answered her door in a pink robe with pink rollers in her hair, no shoes or socks on, showing off her pink toenails along with her pink fingernails.

"Miss did you call concerning a domestic dispute?" One of the three offices standing outside her door asked.

Speaking ghetto with a trace of attitude and a little bit of neck action while bobbing her head yeah, she said. "Um-uhn. Y'all came quick for a change but not quick enough. That sorry motherfucker been gone."

Looking at each other, the lead officer asked. "Miss what did you say his name was again for verification?"

"Julius Pringleton. That's that nigga's name. He came hitting on me, jacking me up and shit. He cursing and mad, putting his fucking hands on me because I didn't let him in my house the other night," she said talking more with her hands. "We may have a child together, but we ain't together. He needs to accept that. I don't got to open my door for nobody if I don't want to."

Nana kept going on and on but the police was only concerned about one thing. "What night was this he popped up?"

"About three days ago. I had company and wasn't in the mood for him and all his bullshit."

"Ms. Wilson you have no idea where he might be?"

Mad and infuriated beyond reasons that she gave the police, *I'mma teach his no good trifling ass a lesson today about putting his broke hands on me. So what if I'm fucking his friend, the nigga taking care his baby and this my pussy, I fuck who I want to*, she thought. So she told police, "Probably in that crackhead Camilla's apartment. Building 106."

Noticing that the police weren't taking notes of what she was saying, she was about to ask "What's up with that," but the officer said after getting off his walkie-talkie, "Ms. Wilson, would you step aside please ma'am. We have to search your house."

"Search my house!" She shouted in astonishment. "For what? The nigga hit me."

"I hate to have to tell you this but I presume you don't already know. Mr. Singleton is wanted for a murder that happened in the market three nights ago," he paused to let his next words sink in. "The same night you say he was beating on your door. Now if you move aside, we can be out just as quickly as we have come, otherwise we'll be forced to enter your home physically."

Using her hands to cover her mouth, shocked from what she just heard and realizing she just handed over her child's father straight to the police, Nana stood in disbelief as the three police officers searched her home.

Sitting in her living room watching the eight o'clock movie on the Lifetime channel and listening to Trimpell's new self, Kellyn realized that she has foreseen these events happening. Placing a child in a loose environment and that child was bound to become loose. Some things are just inevitable. She provided for Trimpell every need, kept up with his schooling, which is how she found out his behavior in class was pretty much the same whenever he was in class, which is more less than often. She knew his grades were dropping and she knew it was his environment rubbing off on him. Still she pressured him to do better. If Eisha could've seen the changes her baby was undergoing, she would have been jumped out of her grave. In fact, she wanted to tell him that, as she did her best to discipline him through the phone, but she hated to bring it up. It would've been reopening old wounds that never heal.

Trimpell must have guessed her thoughts because his next words were, "I miss my mama," he said.

Instantly she felt his heart beating through the phone as his voice cracked. She wanted to cry for him at this moment like she did many nights. She really feels and sees exactly what he's going through. Staying strong, she told him, "I know, Trimppy, but you have to stay strong, baby. Your mom is always in your heart even when you think she's not."

Hearing the hurt and anger in his voice when he said, "Things were different when she was here." She forgot about the movie on TV and spoke into the phone as if she was standing right there in front of Trimpell, for she knew how so true for him his words were. "Oh baby, you're right. Things were different but you don't have to change now that she's not here. Stay the same ol' good Trimpell she wants you to be, like I want you to be, because we both love you." She said hoping her love means something to him. His next words sent a flame of love through her whole body. His voice reminded her of the Trimpell she gave the nickname Trimppy to so many years ago.

"Can I come with you?"

Hopping straight off her couch, dropping the remote out of her lap to get something on real quick to protect her from the cool night breeze, she said, "Sure you can." She noted to herself this will be the first time she will get Trimpell since Eisha died. "Go tell your auntie right now, that you're coming with me. And pack yourself a bag full of clothes."

Happy that he was getting a bit of relief, Trimpell got up from the bottom step and asked, "Really Kell Bell?" He heard her say, "I'm grabbing my keys right now," and excitedly he ran out from the closed confines of the apartment hallway.

"Freeze!" He heard someone tell him. Quickly looking and seeing a silhouette of a tall white officer with his gun drawn in the night sky headed his way.

Trimpell took his hand holding the phone and touched the pocket he had the piece of blunt in, turned on his heels and ran.

"He's got a gun," another voice called out, seeing something in his hand. "Suspect armed and fleeing," the officer radioed in.

Hearing wind cutting through the phone and what seemed like a commotion, Kellyn called out to him, "Trimpell!" and got no answer. Listening and trying to hear what was going on, Kellyn heard several voices yelling what sounded like "Freeze!" and "Don't move!"

Trimpell was halfway up the apartment steps when the officers turned into the hallway. The last words he heard was "Drop the gun!"

Faw! A single shot sounded off, followed by a barrage of gunshots. *Blaw blaw faw faw faw*!

"Cease fire, cease fire," the only black officer hollered but it was too late. Trimpell went stumbling down the stairs, landing on his face. "Cease fire!" he yelled a third time knowing it was too late. Hurt by the lack of respect his fellow officers have for his own people's lives—black lives. To them, it didn't matter. If you're black, you're guilty.

Kellyn heard the gunshots then the sound of Trimpell's phone hitting the ground and getting disconnected. She cried into the phone, "Trimpell!" and ran to her car.

Faw!

The first gunshot startled Camilla's high. It was too close for comfort. She hopped out of her bed, crack pipe still in her hand and walked into her living room, checking every room as she passed and conducting a head count. There were only four heads. Bless and his homeboy sat on her couch, smoking a blunt of weed out a big sack of ganja that sat on her coffee table and her two sons lying on the floor, playing the PlayStation. "Where is Trimpell?" she asked concerned. The look on everyone's faces sent her running to the door. Bless tried to stop her.

"Girl people out there shooting. Don't carry your ass out there."

Scared, not knowing what was going on outside her door, she said, "Nigga get your fucking hands off me. My nephew's outside somewhere."

Through gritted teeth, Bless blocked her path out the door and spoke, "Don't carry your crackhead ass out this house."

Oddly, the feeling that something was terribly wrong was strong in her mind and in her stomach. Knowing she couldn't overpower Bless out of her way, she jabbed him in the eye with her crack pipe. "Ow, you stupid bitch!" He doubled over, clutching his eye. Quickly, she shot a kick to his crotch, causing him to buckle to the floor and she pushed him out her way and ran outside into the hallway. As soon as she passed her threshold to her home, she stopped dead in tracks. Not because white men were aiming guns at her screaming, "Don't move!" but because Trimpell was lying facedown on the steps, in a very awkward position. Blood was dripping into the concrete cracks below. Instinctively, her hand went to rubbing her scalp as the officers yelled for her to put her hands up. Her bottom lip began to quiver.

Oblivious to what was happening outside the door, Bless charged out the house in a rage and tackled Camilla hard into the door across from hers, knocking her completely out. Leaning on her, about to assault her further, he heard "Freeze!" and looked back to find guns pointed dead on his face, then to Camilla's nephew's body as his partner and Camilla's two sons stood in the doorway looking on.

"Julius Singleton, put your fucking hands up. You're under arrest."

Rounding the corner to Camilla's apartment building, it looked like the whole apartment complex was there, watching what was taking place. Kellyn hopped out of her car in the middle of the road, unable to park at Camilla's building and speedily parted the crowd till she got to the yellow tapeline where she could see what was going on through all the commotion and flashing lights. She spotted a white sheet laid on the middle of Camilla's stairwell. Her stomach began to bubble looking around for Trimpell. She hated to think it was him under the sheet. But her thoughts grew stronger when she saw Camila off to the side, wailing cries of agony. Ducking under the yellow tape as the officer tried to stop her, she made it to Camilla and knelt down in front of her.

"Them bastards shot and killed him and won't even take his body," she said as Kellyn started to cry also. Kellyn looked at the white sheet and her heart broke as tears fell from her face. "They shot him dead for no reason. Then they took my babies from me." Camila cried.

Kellyn didn't know how to feel at that moment. On the way over she just couldn't stop blaming Camilla. Now seeing her sprawled out in the grass crying like a mad woman who just lost everything she had, she didn't know who was to blame—herself for not demanding Camilla to give up Trimpell, the police who shot him, or the wickedness of the heart of every system, the people of the world.

"It's been a sad day for the city of Charleston, South Carolina, where a nine- year-old African American male was shot to death by a police from the Charleston Police Department. This is Britney Johnson and I'm here at the scene in Bridgeview Apartment Complex in Charleston, South Carolina." She turned around and stuck the microphone toward the large crowd gathered behind her. "Black lives matter! Black lives matter! Black lives matter!" chanted the crowd in the background. "Black lives matter! "Black lives matter!"

"I'm Brittany Johnson, and I will be reporting back to you in just a second."

CHAPTER 12

Since the incident with Mice and Jillian's cousin's passing, B-blue was building with Jillian; he understood his pain and was in the process of molding his anger toward a tangible foe while at the same time getting him ready to talk to God. B-blue kept God knowledgeable of the progress they were making, till it was finally time for them to meet face to face.

Walking up the top tier of the dorm with Jillian a step behind him, B-blue stepped up to Job, Country and Airy who were standing in the hole, a dead end of a hallway with rooms on both sides of the wall and introduced Jillian to them.

"Jillian, this is Country boy, we call him Country." He turned toward Ari. "This is Aryan but we call him Ary for short. And last but not least, this is God." He motioned with his body, stepping out the way so Jillian could see him clearly and gave a slight head nod to Job, "But he goes by Job, like the book in the Bible." Turning toward his brothers he said, "Guys, this is Jillian."

Country, the closest standing to Jillian, nodded his head to him, said "whats up" and stuck out his rock hard fist for Jillian to pound. Pounding his hand on with his knuckles, Jillian thought to himself, *If he'd done it any harder, for sure he would have broken every bone in his hand.*

"What's up?" Ary told him, looking him in eyes. When Jillian returned to jester, he nodded his approval, believing a man wasn't no man if he couldn't look another man in the eyes.

"So it took the death of a loved one from the hands of the other one to bring you home," Job questioned him. "I guess it's true when they say, 'bad thing happens for good reason.' Come." He motioned to his room where they were standing in front of. "Let's talk." Opening the door for Jillian to enter, Job turned to B-blue, Country and Ary and said, "Feel free to get your swords sharpened as well." And they all entered the room, knowing Job was about to bestow some heavy jews on Jillian remembering their first conversation with God.

Inside the room, B-blue sat on top of the locker, while Ari and Country occupied the bed.; Jillian sat at the desk while Job took the center the room floor. "First I heard that you couldn't see," he paused looking at Jillian. "Then I saw that you were blind." He looked over to B-blue. "I said to Blonde and Blue, 'Show him what he can't see with his mind. Show him what he really sees with his eyes.' He came back to me the next day he said, 'Job, I tried.' I told him there's more he can do. He said, 'No, no, Job,' Job imitated B-blue shaking his head no, 'I tried.' I said to him, 'Don't try, strive. Because if you don't, we'll lose him to the other side.' Now here you are! I'm sorry it took what it took to get you here but the fact is you're here. The question I got for you Jillian is, now that you see what's going on, what are you going to do about it? Runback in a nigga's grasp? Let your cousin's passing be in vain? Go spend all your mother's hard-earned cash on niggas, just to get high and fry your fucking brains? Or sharpen your sword and cut these niggas down every chance you get. 'Cause as I now hope you see, a nigga don't give a fuck about you." Job pierced Jillian's eyes with his own. If it was true the eyes are the gateway to your soul, then Job was steering into Jillian's. "No they don't give a fuck about any of us here. How could they care about you, me, him, or our people when they don't care about themselves, their own kind. The truth I tell it, I swear. Look at them, they steal from each other, they rob each other, kill each other, and when they get caught and go to jail, they tell on each other," he paused for the right effect of his words, "to our police system. Backstab each other to our police system." Job made sure he had much emphasis on all his words. "They are people without hearts. Look at the way they live," Job started to fire off examples of their living conditions, "In poverty, section eight, government housing, in projects, ghettos, and hoods. Think about it," he told them, "all those are nothing more than plantation's slave quarters and shacks. We," he tapped himself on the chest, "and our government knows this. We knew if we didn't give them a place to live, they would sleep on the streets. If we didn't give them welfare, EBT, they wouldn't work to feed themselves, their children. See they're heartless and careless. They have no determination, they're desireless. They don't even want to do better for themselves. Yeah they can uplift themselves, but we know that they won't. So it's our job to make it harder for them whenever they get the urge to do better, which will eventually lead to them opposing us. We're not supposed to help them.

"Whenever you ride through their ghettos and hoods, you see fast food on every corner. The same shit that's killing them by the second, giving them heart failure and diabetes. Liquor stores on every corner, drugs on every corner, bums and hookers, AIDS on every corner. We did that to keep them reflecting what they see, so they can waste their time fighting their environment, their circumstances, themselves, instead of us. The truth I tell it, I swear. And this ain't even half of it, not even a quarter of it.

"See, we know who they really are, that's why we must keep them down. That's why we send them to our schools, our institutions from the age of six to eighteen. The years the child's mind develops the most. Fill up their left brain with what we say is the truth. Our history. And by doing so, we dictate their reality, their future. Cutting them off from their right brain, their Higher Selves, their godly selves. In our schools, we teach them how to work our jobs, manage our businesses, become selective stewardess, slaves of their choice at their own will."

Tapping his chest he said, "We are supreme. In their churches, they pray to our Jesus, our God. We gave them Christianity. Our God and Jesus, black or white, will never be a savior for them. We are the only reason they have faith. We gave them belief, we gave them truth," he said, still tapping his chest then out of nowhere, he heard keys behind him opening his room door.

"You boys alright in here? I sure hear a lot of yelling." The older black female officer stuck her head in the room.

"Yes ma'am Ms. Mary. We're alright," Job said changing his whole tone. "Are you doing alright tonight?"

"My sugar's bothering me a little bit but I'll be alright. I know God got my back. Now y'all boys have a nice evening and try to keep it down in here okay for Ms. Mary. I don't need none of superiors coming down on me about noise . . ." Officer Mary said and exited the room just as quietly and quickly as she entered.

As she closed the door, Job mumbled, "Black bitch." Turning back to his audience, who was listening to him intently, he said, "Like I was saying before we were rudely interrupted, I know you can clearly see there is a war going on between us and them. I know it sounds like we're winning and maybe we are, but it's not an easy fight. We're all we got and they outnumbered us ten to one in the world. But here in America, we make up about 80 percent of the population. We need every soldier we can get and everyone we can't get, is useless to us—dead weight. Now again I ask you, 'What are you going to do about it? Whose side are you on?'"

Manipulated to feel alone inside the penitentiary, that the blacks were his enemies and his old kind was the only ones who would look out for him, care for him, stand up for him, Jillian drew himself into the world of supremacy. Slowly but surely, he started talking to B-blue, building on history more at night after lockdown. He presented Job with racial questions like, "Why do blacks like to say they were here first?" just so he could preach to him. He started checking out books on Aryan supremacy, studying Hitler. He would chill with Country so he could point out the war on blacks that was happening in America. Job kept preaching about the news to him. Everything he seemed to be doing was bringing him closer to what they called home, his true self, his Aryan self.

Taking it a bit further after a month of being indoctrinated, Jillian started to work out with them regularly, gaining more indoctrination into the 1 percent. "That's it, pull," Ary motivated Jillian as he did his set of pull-ups outside on the rec field. "One more, ten. There you go, good money." Jillian released the pull-up bar he was hanging from and dropped to the ground, feeling exhausted from straining himself.

"Whoa." He said exasperated. "These pulls are not to be played with. I know I'm going to be sore the morning," he said while bent over, hands on his knees, and taking a deep breath.

"No pain, no gain. Soreness is a good thing," Country told him, then hopped up on the bar and knocked out his ten pull-ups with ease.

B-blue ended their set of pull-ups when he came down from the bar, and Job announced their last exercise for the afternoon.

"Thirty laps!" Jillian shouted looking at the perimeter of the rec field. "That's a lot of damn laps."

"And we bout to jog each one of them, so come." And Job took off telling them, "Pick your own pace, just no walking. Now let's go." He cheered them on as they all followed behind them.

Six more laps, Jillian thought. They finished seven laps ago as they waited off to the side and pushed him on. On his last go around completing his thirty laps, he fell to the ground where they stood.

Dripping in sweat and breathing fast, repetitively, Job told him, "Your body is your temple. Constantly you must purify and strengthen it. Likewise with your mind. A weak body is the image of a weak mind. So a strong mind manifests a strong body and vice versa."

Taking the ground next to him and relaxing his body he continued, "The heavy breathing, sweat and fatigue are good for you, for us all. All these chemicals we intake, unhealthy food, drugs," he looked at Jillian who was the only one indulging in consuming drugs amongst them, "is coming out of you. You're purifying yourself, taking care of yourself. Now it does no good for you to cleanse yourself just to go back and put in the same things that's killing you, back inside of you." Looking around to make sure he was out of earshot from the other inmates on the rec field, he leaned in closer to Jillian but spoke loud enough for Country, B-blue and Ari to hear, he said "That's what niggers do or white niggers, crackers. You're not a nigger or a cracker right, which means an ignorant person? A person who hates himself and neglects himself places drugs into himself, thus, weakening himself instead of strengthening himself, mentally and physically. A person loves what they take care of. So love yourself, don't hate yourself Jillian."

Jillian nodded his head up and down as she listened to Job preach.

Job thought about all that his people were losing to hating themselves and he shook his head. "Hate is powerful. It's the opposite of love, the most powerful energy in the universe. Hate is something we all do, something we can't avoid but can control and direct. So we must redirect that hate from ourselves to someone who deserves it, them. Think of how much stronger us as a people would be, if we weren't hating ourselves. Destroying ourselves with the drugs, with meth. Think about it because our government sure is. They can't put up a sign up saying, "Hey, white people, our plan backfired on us. Meth was invented for them, but they rejected it and you accepted it. Now get off it because it's killing you epidemically."

"So look around you." Job looked in the direction of all the white inmates scattered about on the rec field, which was everywhere. "This is what they do. Implement new drug laws. And take a wild guess Jill Jill, for who."

"For them?" He asked more than answered.

"For them!" Job cried. "Fuck no, not for them. We've been punching them for drugs since they started to sell it. Prison been over packed with blacks since the 60s behind drugs. Now with this meth scenario affecting us, they dropped 85 percent on all drug charges. Implemented new programs in the penitentiaries that guarantees parole under the disguise for everybody. This the program." He said still looking over all of the white inmates. "Look around you, who do you see? Us. Look at the demographics of the penitentiary; 70 percent black, 25 percent white and 5 percent others. Now look at the demographics of this program; 7 percent black, 3 percent others and 90 percent Caucasian."

Coming to an end in his speech Job said, "They need us in this battle Jillian, strong physically and strong mentally. They need us supreme. They're telling us by showing us, but it's up to us to get there."

Getting up from the ground where he sat with Jillian, Job said, "Come on. Rec about to close, let's beat these niggers and crackers to the shower."

New York City

"This has got to stop!" A middle-aged black mother of two adolescent boys said into the microphone the news reporter was holding to her mouth. "I have just witnessed the most horrible thing my eyes have ever seen in my entire life. Those six officers," the mother pointed in the direction where all the police officers on scene had gathered up, "murdered that man in cold blood. All he said was, 'for what' and they hollered resisting arrest and hopped on that man. I told them to stop, they're hurting that man. He was telling them he's not resisting, to stop, we all were telling them to stop. Then the guy they brutally murdered started to heave out the words, 'I can't breathe.' I was close enough to hear it, so the officers had to hear it. But what did they do, they didn't stop. They killed him in plain sight. In front of women, in front of children, in front of the world. And these are the people who are supposed to protect and serve. Last week it was Sandra Bland, Michael Brown, Tamira Rice, Walter Scott, Trayvon Martin. A child, they're killing children, babies. The little boy Trimpell down in Charleston, South Carolina. Innocent kids. Black lives matter. All lives matter. This is a disgrace, a slap in the face and it needs to stop. The 2000s is turning into the 1950s and 60s all over again.

"No, we are not going back into our homes. No we will not leave the streets, no we are not rioting, we are protesting, fighting for our rights. We want justice and we want equality!"

"I'm Brittany Johnson," the news reporter said as the cameraman panned the camera toward her. "Here in New York City where protesters are gathered in front of a corner store behind what appears to be another badge-on-black death. Witnesses say six officers screamed resisting arrest and ended up strangling a store owner to death while trying to place him in custody. Witnesses say the victim told the officers he couldn't breathe several times before he passed away. This has been another tragic incident, another life loss. I'm Britney Johnson reporting for Channel 10 News."

"Look at this shit," Jillian said concentrating on the news, watching from B-blue's small TV in their room, causing everybody to take a look at what he was looking at. "Six cops just strangled some nigga out in New York."

"Another one bites the dust." Country said nonchalantly.

"We're on a roll boys," Airy cheered excitedly, slapping Jillian on his back. "That's like the eleventh or twelfth nigger that got killed by the police," he told Jillian. "In three months. We're in the heat of the battle."

B-blue nodded his head in agreement to Ary's assessment while Country and Jillian made similar references to what was going on and Job stared at the TV without a crack of a smile on his face, knowing these times had been prophesied in Revelations; the shootings, wars, famine, the rise in homosexuality. Realizing the seriousness of what was really going on, he cleared it all up for them. "This is the beginning of Armageddon. The final battle between good and evil. It has been prophesied that all evil forces will be destroyed. This my brothers, is the Apocalypse. Only the good and the pure shall survive."

CHAPTER 13

Charleston, South Carolina

"Hello?" Chris answered his phone solemnly.

Hearing his baby brother's tone sound so depleted of life, Tommy hoped to awaken him out of his somber as he poured himself a drink in his home after a good day of work followed by plenty of paperwork. "I got some good news, hopefully music to your ears." Whispering on the phone he said, "I killed me a coon today. I shot him seven times for trying to take my Taser."

Shifting his position in the bed where he was lying down, Chris sat up as he listened to his brother brag about killing somebody. "He tried to take your Taser. That's crazy."

"It's payback, that's what it is," Tommy said feeling the burn of the liquor go down in his chest. "Clean and easy payback. Hell, all over the world people are catching coons and killing them. I might as well get me one too." He joked and laughed.

Chris thought to himself, *I should catch a couple niggas and kill them too, after all they took from me. Maybe I'll feel a bit better.*

Things just weren't the same nowadays by himself. Every step, every word, every thought, every place he went, felt different now that Chrissy was gone and her death added so much more to losing Carol a year earlier. He was literally in shambles.

"Yeah me too Tommy." He told his brother in the same somber tone. "Hey listen man, I'm a little tired right now. Let's talk about this a little bit later." He said, not in the mood for conversing. He just wanted to find shade in his shadows, peace in his memories.

"Chris, it's been three months now," Tommy told him, unable to cheer him up. "You got to keep pushing bro. I know you miss her. I miss her, we all miss her." Catching himself he said, "We all miss them both. But you got to move on. They're gone and you're here. They wouldn't want you shackled up in the house all day, moping and killing yourself with stress. No they would want you standing up for them, defending them in their death."

Tired of being lectured to, he laid back down on his bed with one hand still holding the phone and his other hand on his forehead. He knew that was the last thing they both would want. There wasn't a vengeful bone in their bodies.

"How about you come and work with me? I can get you on the job. You know who the chief of police is. The power of the badge is amazing. Your words become law against theirs. Fill out a little bit of paperwork and what you say stands up. Do you hear what I'm telling you? Chris! I just killed a fucking coon today. Look at what's going on in the world. Join the badge Chris and together, me and you can hunt those bastards down and peel the black off their bodies." Tommy said, obviously wired up from the liquor and left-over rush of adrenaline flowing through his body from killing a man in cold blood and getting away with it.

Tommy's suggestion didn't sound too bad, but that wasn't what he wanted. What he wanted was his wife and child back. He wanted to be able to sleep at night in the spoon position—he and Carol entwined together. He wanted to feel the comfort of his daughter's love and presence one more time. What he wanted was to have another chance to share life with them, knowing if he could, he would do it differently; he would do it with love.

"Hello? Chris you there?" Tommy kept saying into the phone, hearing Chris go quiet.

"I'm here Tom-tom. Now just isn't the time. I need to sort some things out, regroup. I'm coming along, it's just taking time, that's all. Time to find out what to do next. I keep blaming everyone and everything else for what's going on and it's not satisfying me. I need answers Tommy. Why did I lose my family?"

"You know who's to blame Chris, these fucking niggers."

"I know." Chris said but blaming niggers wasn't it.

"That's why you lost your loved ones. I tell you this fool. You can sit around and mope all damn day, but those bastards took my niece away from me and I'm going to take as many of them as I can to hell with me."

Click. Tommy hung up dead in Chris's ear.

Tossing his cell phone on the bed beside him, Chris stared at the ceiling, hating to accept the truth of his situation. The truth Carol told him was going happen. It was him who was to blame.

'Sympathy where are you at?' The text came from her best friend Shema while she was in the middle of class.

"Bitch I'm in the middle of minding my own business 101. What the hell do you want?" she texted back quickly.

"Girl go to my page and look what they're posting on Facebook. SMH!" Shema replied.

"This better be good Shema. Exams are on Friday," she texted Shema then quickly hid her phone knowing Professor Xavier hated phones in his classroom.

Minimizing the current window on her laptop and opening her Facebook account, Sympathy went to Shema's FB page and looked at her Timeline. Her most recent post was titled "N. Charleston Cop Plants Taser on Victim" with 32,011 likes in two hours. This had to be it. She clicked on it to play and a video showed a man struggling with a police officer and breaks away.

"Hey!" A classmate blurted out sitting behind her getting a full glimpse of what she was viewing. "That's the shooting that took place yesterday on Remount Road." He said out loud.

"What's that Mr. Frayer?" Professor X asked while he approached him after being interrupted by his outburst.

"The shooting that was on the news. A cop shot a man on Remount Road. Look!" He pointed to Sympathy's computer.

"Ms. Songs, what is it you're observing. Why is Mr. Frayer interrupting my class?"

Having watched the whole video, Sympathy faced the laptop his way and replayed it for him. "Another badge-on-black murder, when is this gonna stop?" she asked to no one but everyone.

"Ms. Johnson, I think you should come and see this," one of her assistant journalists chimed, fanning her over to his workstation.

Getting up from her workstation and heading to his, she asked irritated, "What is it Gary?"

"232,000 Likes and 520,000 comments in 7 hours."

"Seven hours!" Brittany exclaimed. "What is it?" she asked.

"Cold-blooded cops."

On paid leave from yesterday's event, Tommy was standing outside in his front yard with a beer in hand while smoking a cigarette and watering his garden when he heard police Cruisers pull up simultaneously, disturbing the peace in broad daylight in his quiet suburban neighborhood.

Turning around, he saw the tactical team stopped directly in front of his house and hopped out just as quickly as they stopped with their guns drawn and yelling obscenities in his direction. This was the last thing he expected to see as the water hose fell from his hand along with the beer can in his other hand. His jaw dropped, leaving the cigarette hanging from his bottom lip as the water hose muddied the ground he was standing on.

"Put your fucking hands up." A black officer he had never seen before in tactical gear screamed at him.

Realizing the cigarette was dangling from his lip, he went to grab it as the tactical team approached him.

"Keep your fucking hands up," the same man yelled inches away from him with the barrel to his Heckler and Koch AR15 dead in his face. "Or I will blow your fucking brains out white boy. Get on the fucking ground and keep your fucking hands up" He instructed Tommy.

"I can't," Tommy started, but as if knowing what he was going to tell him, the man in tactical gear said, "Then drop to your fucking knees and keep 'em up," he yelled as he assisted him to his knees, then face first in the muddy ground.

With a knee on his back holding him immobile, Officer Scott and three other officers then proceeded to handcuff him as he was read his rights.

Bending over to pick him up off the ground, the head of the tactical team Officer Scott whispered in his ear, "How does it feel to be on other side of the badge coon killer?" Marking the words he heard Officer Tommy Cooper used in the tapped conversation with his brother. *Stupid motherfucker knew he was under investigation*, thought Officer Scott as he picked him up off the ground. He looked at Tommy with all the mud face and told him, "You should see yourself. You look like one of us now."

Chris strolled down the aisles of the grocery store, shopping, buggy devoid of interest due to his life being devoid of Chrissy. They would go shopping together and Chrissy would have the buggy full of all kinds of irregular choices of food and snacks, bringing out exotic flavors in him. She would want brownies, he would want cookies. Undecided on what they would get, they always ended up getting both and cooked them together. She would want pop tarts and he would get hers and find himself a flavor he would like to try. Their buggy would be full of juices, chips, cereals, dips, cheeses of all kind, microwavable quick fixes, hot dogs, and hamburgers and now the buggy only contained eggs, milk, bologna, and potatoes. Nothing was the same without his love.

Searching the raw meat section for a nice healthy steak to eat with his potatoes, the news playing on TV up above on a pedestal catty corner on the wall caught his attention.

"A video clipping of N. Charleston police officer shooting an unarmed man has gone viral. Apparently a couple of kids recorded the shooting with their cell phone and uploaded it on Facebook." The TV screen then showed an officer gunning a man down as he ran away from him.

Chris became light-headed in an instant. He knew it was his brother.

Next the news reporter came back on with a picture of his brother. "Officer Tommy Cooper is being charged with first degree murder as well as obstruction of justice and could be possibly facing other charges as well. This is Britney Johnson with Channel 10 News."

Stuck staring at the TV as it went blank, Chris saw his wife and daughter in the reflection of the screen, both dressed in the white dresses they were buried in, both embracing each other and both staring back at him.

He was to blame for their death. His hate is what took them out of his life and he finally was coming to realization of it seeing what his brother's hate did to him.

"Hate is an energy Chris and all it does is bring what you hate into your life." Carol told him.

"Hate plus hate only equals twice the hate. Stop hating Daddy. Love is the answer. You got to learn to love 'cause we love you." Chrissy said.

Then Carol told him three words she always meant with all her heart, "always and forever." And then she blew him a goodbye kiss as Chrissy waved by to him.

Britney Johnson came back on the screen and Chris broke down in tears knowing he was to be blamed for his wife, his daughter, his family, his brother, and himself. Tears flooded his eyes as they poured down his cheeks.

Seeing a crying man as she approached the raw meat section of the supermarket, Ms. Alice Gladden approached him with caution. "Sir are you alright?" She asked placing her lower hand on his back.

Uncovering his face with his hands as tears continue to fall, Chris saw the elderly black woman, heard real compassion in her voice and saw it on her face for him, a white man she knew nothing about, and he cried harder realizing that his whole life he was wrong. He hated blacks his whole life for no reason. He hated them out of ignorance. "I'm sorry." He reached out to her and hugged her as tightly as her frail body could take, crying on her shoulder as she held him back like a mother holds her child. "I'm so, so sorry for everything. Please forgive me?" He pleaded to her, feeling she understood what he was apologizing for and she did. Words weren't needed to explain a person's heart when God gave us all the power of intuition.

Rubbing him on his back as he cried, Miss Alice Gladden told him, "It's gonna be okay son. You could apologize to me a thousand times and I could forgive you a thousand times but you only need to apologize to God once. All you gotta do is pray baby. Just pray."

CHAPTER 14

Since that fatal day when all she had to live for were taken from her, Camilla has given up on life and her well-being. She began to do any and everything she could to get high. The government gave her a sixty-one dollar check every month to pay her water bill and another forty-eight-dollar check for her rent, yet her water was cut off and she was on the verge of being homeless because those checks along with her EBT went to the purchase of drugs.

Next it was her furniture, Trimpell's PlayStation and games, everything she could sell got sold, not excluding her body which has shriveled to skin and bones. No longer having children to feed, she stopped feeding herself. Her only intake was crack cocaine.

Then the monkey possessed her. He was on her back and in her head, sending her visions of her nephew lying dead on her apartment steps. He hurt her. He sent another vision of Trimpell's blood dripping on the concrete floor below her steps. "I'm going to make you or break you," the monkey said into her head, hurting her as he took her back to the way the police left his body out for everyone to see. "You know what Eisha's only dream was? You diminished it." He continued to torment her, ripping her from the inside out. "That's not enough for you." He showed her a vision of Trimpell, Richie and Rayquan playing PlayStation 4 in her living room. Then slowly Trimpell disappeared, then Richie, then Rayquan. "Where your boys at?" He chastised her. "Who you going to curse out now for stealing your lighters? Who you going to cook for?"

"You're killing me!" She said to herself.

"No, I'm not killing you. Losing your kids and nephew killed you. I'mma bring you back to life. Go find some of me, monkey nuts and smoke me. Don't fight me. Find me and smoke me. You need me."

"Come on Nessa," Camilla stood inside the hallway of her bare apartment, begging a female hustler from the complex. Camilla was being kicked out of the apartment on the first of the month if she didn't get her lights turned back on and her rent paid. "Give me a hit, I need it bad girl." She said almost in tears as she stood hunched over using the wall to support her frail body and scratching her arm. "We go way back. You know what happened to me Nessa. They killed my nephew and took my kids. Nessa I need it bad. Please!" She looked deep into her eyes as she held both her palms up. "I'll," she stuttered, ashamed of what she was about to say to her one true friend, "I'll eat your pussy."

Nessa was shocked Camilla would offer to do such a thing to her. Standing inside her empty apartment, deplete of everything but the carpet on the floor, she cocked back her hand to slap Camilla but stopped as she took in her once upon a time babysitter, looking like a sick and totally different person and felt a whole range of mixed emotions for her. Shaking her head no in disbelief, dropping her hand back to her side she said, "Camilla I ought to slap the shit out of you," She jumped at her like she was about to hit her, "for saying something like that to me. No, I ought to slap the shit out of you for doing this to yourself."

"I know, I know," Camilla said, nodding her head.

"No, you don't know 'cause if you did, you won't be asking to eat a bitch's pussy. Camilla you ain't gay. This shit," she produced a bag of crack in her hand "took your kids, your nephew, yourself away from you, your soul." Hearing the truth brought tears to Camilla's eyes. "Girl the state just killed your nephew and the same motherfuckers got your kids and you got the nerve to be around here begging for crack. You a stupid black bitch." She placed the bag in her face and shook it. "What's wrong with you? What about li'l Richie and Rayquan? Lil Dreadhead misses those boys. He asks me every day, "Mama when they coming back?" and I don't know what to tell him. I see the hurt in his eyes and I hurt not only for them, him, or for myself, but for you to Camilla. Since you let this shit get the best of you, huh." She threw the bag on the floor in front of her spilling some of the rocks out of the bag. "It might as well get the rest of you. Smoke to your heart's bust." She turned to leave then stopped in her tracks and looked back at Camilla, catching her grabbing up the crack. "I remember when you first got Trimppy. You told me about that woman who wanted to get him from you." She softly shook her head as she recollected. "You talked all that shit about that lady because she was white. Bitch, it was that same white woman who was holding your ass that night he got killed, crying with your sorry ass. Well, the real white woman got your kids now and your people ain't doing a damn thing for you. If you don't die in here tonight, I'll bet you it'll be the same white woman who would do all she can to help your stupid black ass." Then she continued her stride out of what was left of Camilla's home.

With the lit candle being her only source of light, Camilla gathered all the pieces of crack that fell out of the bag Nessa threw at her. She knew Nessa was going to look out for her, but not like this. She counted eighteen to twenty rocks and with her stem being in her robe pocket. She didn't bother to smoke in her room where she normally smoked. She sat right there on what used to be her living room floor and got high, loading whole rocks onto her stem, trying to bust her heart so she wouldn't have to feel no more pain.

Seven hours later, her throat was sore from smoking all eighteen rocks and she was crawling on her hands and knees, searching her carpet with the candle hoping to find more crack rock. Picking something up off the carpet and tasting it, checking to see if it was a piece of crack, Camilla tossed whatever it was, accidentally knocking over her only source of light, the candle. "Shit!" she cursed, trying to save it, but it was too late. The wick blew out.

Falling back on her bony behind, she smiled, forgetting her bigger situation due to being high. The only thing on her mind was getting another light from her neighbor, who kept looking at her strangely every time she came and asked for something. Thinking of why he kept looking at her brought it all back. She was a disgrace to him.

Her mind ran to her kids. In the blackness of her apartment, she could see them, but knew it was only her mind playing tricks on her. Bringing her hands to her face, she felt something she forgot was there, her stem. Instantly she wanted to get high again. The memories of her kids wouldn't stay away. She thought of her nephew. As the blackness in the room turned into light, a figure, a person came through the light out of the blackness. "Camilla girl, what are you doing to yourself?" Seeing her dead sister Eisha made her jump and back away straight into the wall. "Some things you can't run from baby girl. And trying to will only destroy you."

"Eisha?" Camilla's voice quivered as she asked, "What you doing here?"

"I have come to save you Camilla from destroying yourself. It's not taking the pain away." Eisha shook her head no. "It's only making the pain worse and it's only making what you are going through more painful. It's not going to get your kids back. It's going to keep them from you."

"Oh Eisha." Camilla started to cry with her fist so tight, it crushed her crack pipe in her hand. "I'm sorry!"

Knowing what she was sorry for Eisha said, "Don't worry girl, my baby is doing just fine."

And out of the light came Trimpell, running till he stopped and clutched onto his mother. "It's not your fault Aunty. God took me so he could save you and now you can save Richie and Rayquan." He told her this as he snuggled in his mother's embrace.

"Okay!" Camilla cried, nodding her head in understanding, knowing what she must do. "Okay."

"This is the end Camilla." Eisha said, backing up into the light with Trimpell. "Your Armageddon, your final battle between good and evil, right and wrong. Don't let my baby's last breath be in vain." Eisha said right before she disappeared and in a last speck of light Camilla saw what she was looking for, a piece of crack rock. Thinking her mind was playing another trick on her, she reached for it and grabbed it. Not having to inspect it, she knew from its texture what it was, but oddly she didn't desire it. She just held it in her hands thinking. Then she lifted her other hand equal to her hand with the crack in it, tried to open her fist and felt the pain of the broken glass stem in her palm and sighed out in agony as she continued to open her hand. She couldn't see nothing, but knew her palm was busted open. She became furious! Not at the fact her pipe was broken, but at the fact of how it broke her. In a rage, she cocked back her closed fist and threw the crack out her hand as she yelled a mad woman's fury, bringing tears out her eyes. Oblivious to the broken grass in her hand, she pushed herself up off the ground with both hands and wildly she ran to the front door, snatching it open, ignoring the raw pain in her palm as she touched the doorknob, still yelling from her fury. She took the flight of stairs down her apartment steps and fled out into the streets in the wee hours of the morning.

Not knowing where she was going, Camilla just ran away from what she called life. She ran long and hard, out the complex, past the graveyard and onto the main highway. She just kept running, motivated by her sisters and nephew's spirit. She ran till she lost her breath and her footing, falling face down on the ground.

Camilla laid there till she found the willpower to get up and when she did, she realized she was in the middle of Meeting Street extension. Refusing to go back, she looked up ahead and saw the sign, "The pantry." With nowhere else to go, that's where she was slowly headed, in the empty streets as she walked away from her old ways.

Exceedingly tired from a very long day at work, Lisa sat in the pantry's office, unwinding herself, till the 2:00 a.m. shift came on, allowing the new girl to serve the few customers that came into the store. Slightly dosing in the office chair, the chime of the bell alerting her that someone entered the store, brought her back to life. She studied the camera's monitor to stereotype the customer, if he was a suspect or not, for these hours were the hours of travelers, club goers, robbers, and killers. Lisa saw an unthreatening-looking black guy, middle-aged, walking down aisle 3.

Leaning back on her chair about to reclaim her doze, she spotted him grab a handful of crackers and stuffed them into his pants' pocket right before she was about to take her eyes off the camera. *Not tonight*, she thought as she sat up, not wanting to confront him by herself jeopardizing the lives of her and her employee, and grabbed the phone to call the police. Having done this a million times, she switched to the camera outside to get the plate numbers of the car he was driving. Zooming in on the back of the car, she saw someone move in the back window. With further inspection she saw three kids that couldn't be no more than seven years old. *Crackers*! she thought, as she hesitated to press the nine button. Curiosity got the best of her and she switched the camera back to inside the store and caught the man stealing sandwiches out the cooler. Swiveling in her chair, she looked out to the door of her office, to her cashier and made a mental note to speak with her about talking less on the phone and paying more attention to the store.

Rationalizing what he was doing and seeing the kids in the car, she deduced they must be hungry and he was broke. For assurance that she was doing the right thing, by letting him get away with his stolen goods, as she hung up the phone in her hand, Lisa got up to take the register. The cashier hung up the phone and the customer came up from the back of the store with the fifty-cent juice in his hand. "Would this be all?" Lisa asked.

Digging into his pockets and dropping a handful of change on to the counter, he said, "I would like some gas too." And began counting out the few quarters, dimes and nickels. "Uh, just forget about the drink. I'll just put all this on pump seven. Three dollars and twenty-two cents." He told her.

Assured now that she made the right decision, Lisa told him, "Take the drink too." Then scooped up the change and dropped it into the register. Thinking; '*I would do the same to feed my kids too.*' Seeing the man question her authenticity, she dug into her own pockets and produced two quarters. "Have a nice morning, sir."

When he was out the store she said to her cashier, "Pay more attention to the store even if it means staying off that phone some. That man just stole enough to feed a family." Seeing the expression on her face, Lisa said, "Usually I'll have thieves arrested and placed where they need to be but tonight," she shrugged her shoulders, "I may have had an epiphany on life and I think I'm going to start living it differently."

"Wow!" The cashier emphasized with a surprised expression on her face. "What brought about this change?"

"Something about that guy. He wasn't stealing beer, he was stealing food to feed three kids in his car." Lisa answered, not really sure what brought about her sudden change of heart. "He's not a criminal. He's a father doing what he has to do to feed his kids, a good father." Looking up into her mind she said, "He made me recall an incident a couple of months back. This white guy came into the store with his daughter and physically he assaulted a child, a little boy. And no, I didn't see the entire incident but I tried to figure out what was going on before I even thought about calling the police and he got away. A real criminal. That day I lost a good employee behind the incident and became just as guilty as the man who assaulted that child." Locking eyes with her employee, Lisa said, "I think it's about time I changed my direction and move forward with the world. No one wants to be left behind." She checked her watch, saw it was ten minutes to two in the morning. She said while walking back to the office, "If God ever gives me a chance, I'm going to apologize to that child. I owe him that."

The bell chimed as someone else entered the store.

"How are you doing this morning miss. May I help you?" The cashier said, seeing the raggedy woman approaching her at the register.

"If you may please, I'll be forever indebted to you."

Lisa spun on her heels, hearing the voice of that child she was just speaking of and was stunned to silence when her eyes took him in too.

"I need to go get away from what I used to be. Please, if you can spare me enough money to catch the bus, I promise with my life which is all I got left, I'll repay you. I don't know how but I promise I will." Camilla begged for the realist thing she ever asked for.

Determination isn't just a word, it's an energy and the cashier felt it emanating from this woman as she thought of today's date: 7/7/17; the day of what seems to be transformation, for she was about to change herself as well. Part away with what she held dear, her money, and to a complete stranger. She dug into her pocket and pulled out seven dollars. "Here you go miss. Don't worry about paying me back. Just do what you say you're going to do and I'll be fine."

"Thank you." Camilla gratefully took the money. "You don't know how much this means to me. Thank you, when you see me again you will get your money. I promise you will get your money, thank you!" She said continuously while backing out the store, meaning her every word then looked over to the white woman staring at her in amazement. She nodded her head and got no response and left out the store.

'If I could change Ms. Lisa, we all can change. And if we all can change, then the world could change because we are the world." The cashier looked over to Ms. Lisa who was still staring out the door behind the woman and knew Lisa didn't hear her. "Ms. Lisa?" she was still stuck. "Ms. Lisa?' she called out again a little louder.

The bell chimed and the manager on the next shift entered. "Hey Lisa, look like you just seen a ghost," he said as he patted her on the shoulder and revived her. Taking a deep breath, she heard the cashier. "Hello to Ms. Lisa?" Snapping her fingers. "You didn't hear me?"

"No, what happened?"

"You need to get some rest, that's all. John's here, go home."

Agreeing with her, Lisa nodded her head but had something else in mind, when she saw the woman who just left the store, standing outside in the cold at the bus stop.

"Pretty chilly out here tonight, you might freeze to death waiting on that bus. Where are you headed?" She questioned the woman at the bus stop, pulling up beside her.

Tightly wrapped in her thin robe, Camilla said through chattering teeth, "West Ashley."

"Well hop on in. I can use the company and you sound like you can use the heat." She unlocked her car door.

"Thank you." Camilla entered her car, grateful for the heat.

"Oh it's no problem. I live around that way." Things got silent for a minute as they traveled the morning roads and Lisa's reason for offering this stranger a ride kept nagging her, so she spoke her feelings. "Miss . . ." she started to say and Camilla gave her name. "That's such a beautiful name. Well Ms. Camilla, today has been a long arduous day for me, resulting in a change of life."

"Me too. I'll tell you ms.–" and likewise Ms. Lisa gave her name to Camilla. "Ms. Lisa, me too." Camilla shook her head at her day.

"Maybe that's why we crossed paths. Have you ever heard that whatever intent you have, brings you in contact with people, places, experiences, and opportunities with the same intent?" Camilla said she didn't but immediately she could see the truth in that saying. "Well, we are a living example of it. It wasn't seven minutes before you walked through that door that I decided to change."

Smiling sadly, Camilla said, "Hell, it wasn't seven minutes before I got to that store that I decided to do the same thing."

"Life's amazing like that. Maybe God, something, or someone brought us together. You never know but the fact is here we are, two strangers helping each other, both headed to our new ways of life."

"Seems to me, you're doing all the helping and I appreciate it."

"No Camilla, you're helping me in more ways than we both probably will ever know but the main thing is, your company is keeping me awake and I thank you."

Camilla smiled sensing the genuineness of her claim. "It feels good to know for the first time, I am helping someone. I haven't done that in a long time. I only hurt people."

"Don't beat yourself up about it chile, we all do. I did, I hurt many people, many families. Had plenty people locked up for stealing and the man I should've had arrested, I let him get away for assaulting someone's child, grandchild, somebody's nephew. I let him get away and I'm sorry."

Hearing her speak her soul, Camilla released her own demons as she stared out the car window to the Ashley River as they rode on the Crossgrove Bridge. "It was my ways, my habits, that did me. It got my nephew killed and my kids taken. Still was getting high afterward and

I'm just now realizing that's what it was. Now here I am, finally closing one chapter in my life and starting another one."

"I'm sorry you went through all that Camilla," said Lisa while crossing over into West Ashley.

"Yeah me too. I'm sorry for myself as well."

Lisa asked where to and Camilla answered unsurely like she was taking a leap of faith with nowhere to go. "But I'll tell you this. We're still alive, so we can still can redeem ourselves."

Making eye contact with Lisa, Camilla agreed and said, "We sure can. Yes we sure can." Then mumbled the word redemption.

The rest of their ride was in a comfortable silence until Lisa got the rest of the directions to the home she was dropping Camilla off to. "Well, it was nice meeting you Camilla."

Never realizing white people were so sincere till her ride with Lisa, Camilla said, "The pleasure was all mine." She reached over and hugged her tightly with tears in her eyes.

Before she stepped out, Lisa scribbled down her number and handed it to her. "We came this far together, it doesn't mean it has to end here. Call me if you ever need me, a ride or anything, you call me."

Clutching the paper tightly in her bruised hand, Camilla cried her thanks and watched Lisa pull off. Turning around, she faced her future since her past was behind her. She heard Eisha's voice, "Better late than never." and her faith in what she was about to do was renewed and reaffirmed. She had no idea she was coming here when Lisa asked her "where to" once they were in the West Ashley area. Walking up the steps to the front porch, she lifted her hand to knock on the door, and it just opened for her.

"I couldn't sleep missing them. Then out of the darkness came light and they both appeared to me and told me to open my door". Camilla broke down and started crying as Kellyn grabbed her and together again, they both cried.

CHAPTER 15

Jillian waited patiently outside the video room while the parole board deliberated his faith. A million thoughts ran through his mind as his palms sweat profusely and perspiration formed on his hairless chest. His freedom was being decided by five individuals, two white and three black. The odds were against him.

"Mr. Booth would you step back inside, they're ready for you." An officer opened the door to the video room and told him. His chances were slim to none. "Fuck it!" Jillian thought feeling defeated while taking the seat inside the video room. "Only nine more months to go and they have to release me."

"Mr. Jillian Booth, I, Boe Rally, chairman of the parole board and my counterparts you see on the screen as well has granted you parole on behalf of the state of South Carolina. I advise you to use the remainder of your time in the Department of Correction to further bettering yourself and to prepare for your release on the first next month." Looking at him deeply in the eyes, Boe Rally told him, "Good luck son."

Jillian nodded his head, thanking Joe Rally, saw the white woman nod her head back to him and he returned the gesture. He then caught three black faces staring at him disdainfully. Not a mind reader but he understood their looks. Out of the sixteen people who went up for parole so far today, he was the only one to make it, the only white boy.

Getting up from his seat, he wanted to say into the video camera, "White power!" but thought better of it. What was evident need not be explained. He smiled cheerfully, thanking them all and exited the video room.

Back inside his dorm from his parole meeting and amongst his peers, Jillian couldn't wait to tell them his good news and they couldn't wait to hear it. Expecting him to make it and once it was confirmed he did, they had their own surprise for him.

Gathering up inside his room, Job, B-blue, Airy and Country all took off their shirts and showed their matching tattoos on different body parts. "See Jillian, this is more than a tattoo of a flag, this is a symbol—our symbol—and it stands for what we believe in, what the South believe in and was built on: our superiority. This Confederate flag is a lifestyle we live by. Our ancestors died fighting for this, our separation, our significance. They teach our history at school, it flies at our State House. There will never be equality amongst us. They will always be slaves, and we will always be their masters. And this," Job pointed at his tattoo of the Confederate flag on his chest, "will always represent that. Is this what you stand for?" he asked.

"Fuck yeah!" Jillian shook his head vigorously. "The one percent of the world, my Aryan nation."

"Well take your shirt off. Symbols speak louder than words." Jillian snatched his shirt off his body and B-blue approached him with his tattoo gun in his hand ready to tat. "Where you want it at?"

Thinking about it for a second Jillian said, "You guys picked me up when I fell and brought me to a place I thought was impossible for me to get to in life. You carried me, so I think it's only right I carry the nation on my back."

"Good choice brother. Let's go. Sit on that chair with your back facing me. And remember this, red stands for the blood of our enemies, blue stands for the blood in our bodies, and white stands for the color of our skin."

It took B-blue three hours and forty minutes to tattoo a Confederate flag with a skull head in the middle of it on Jillian's back. "That's bad ass B-blue." Airy said and slapped Jillian on the back.

"Bitch!" Jillian hollered out in pain. "That hurts fuck head."

"It looks good though," Airy told him.

"Let me see, get the mirror," Jillian demanded. B-blue handed him a mirror. "I can't fucking see it.

"Country get the phone," Job told him, "and somebody to snap a picture."

Coming back into the room with the phone and someone to take their picture, Country saw everybody grouped up and striking poses, he gave the phone to their picture taker and went to kneel down in front of them, flexing his bicep to show his tattoo of the Confederate flag and pointed at Jillian's back which was facing the camera. Snap!

"Let me see, let me see." Jillian rushed to look at his art work. Seeing the picture and approving of it, Jillian said, "I'm going to send this to my mom."

April 1, Jillian's release date.

"Oh my god, look at you!" Jillian's mother said, seeing and hugging him for the first time since he left the county jail. Placing kisses all over his face she said, "Your eyes all white, face clean, you even done put on a little weight. Look like you've been taking good care of yourself. Come here and give me another hug before you get in this car." They hugged again.

Foreign to this affection from his mother since he's been a child, Jillian said, "Come on Ma, people watching us." He said, looking at the other families picking their people up from prison as well.

"Let them look. If they love their family like I love my son, they would be doing the same instead of watching us." She said then pinched his cheek. "You look so good. I hope with this new look, you come home with a new attitude."

Jillian smirked thinking, *If she only knew the half of it, she wouldn't ask such a question.* "Come on Mom, let's get out of here. I haven't eaten in days waiting for today."

"Well get in the car. I know you don't want to spend another minute here more than you have to. Shelby's going to be so happy to see you." She said excitedly seeing how good Jillian looked.

Talking the whole ride back to Lexington and through their meal at Golden Corral where they had lunch, Jillian gave her a vivid detail of what prison for him was like. He told her all he did to occupy his time, leaving out one minor detail.

Pulling up to their new home, she said, "Well we're here."

Looking at the two-story home in front of him, Jillian said, "Mom this is nice."

"I know, I know. Neighborhood is better too."

"This place must have cost a fortune." He said more than asked.

"It did but my homeowner insurance helped me out." She gave him a look that reminded him of why she had to get a new home in the first place. "Jill Jill," she said patting him on the thigh, before they hopped out the car, looking into his eyes. "This is your new start. I know I'm not the perfect mom, didn't set the best examples for you but I'm still your mom and no matter what I do, I love you. I do my best for you and want the best for you. Please Jill Jill, I see the changes you said you made in yourself and I'm proud of you. All I ask of you is one thing: please don't go back down that road again. Them drugs and stealing, that's not you. This clean handsome young man I'm seeing now is my son."

Reassuring his mother by squeezing her hand Jillian said to her, "Don't worry Mom. That part of my life is behind me. I'm moving forward. I got a plan and a purpose. I met some real positive people back there Mom and they taught me a lot."

"You just don't know how good I am to hear you speak like that." She pinched his handsome face again. "You just stay focused. I got you a job at a nice country club, starting you off at twelve dollars an hour."

"A country club?" Jillian said

"Yes, a country club. You'll meet plenty of prestigious people and doing the right thing. This place can provide plenty opportunities for you."

"Thanks Mom. I appreciate it."

"You should. I pulled a lot of strings to get you this job. Now come on, let's get inside and let me show you your new room."

Scottish Rite Country Club

Sixteen weeks later

"Hey, you!" one of the assistant managers called out to him. "I been looking all over for you. We're having some important guest today, so I need that dining room spotless. But first, I need you to please park that truck of yours around the back. Looks like you've been bogged inside the mud with that thing."

Jillian wasn't surprised such a request has been made. His Z71 truck did look out of place parked in front of the club along with all the luxury vehicles and foreign cars. He hated to acknowledge this preppy pussy ass cracker, who always gave him a hard time along with the rest of his coworkers, with respect but used to the belittlement Jillian said, "Yes sir!" and proceeded to leave out the kitchen area to move his truck.

Outside in the front parking lot, Jillian saw his truck and the other cars and it reminded him that he too was out of place among Lexington's elite.

His first impression of the country club, seeing it devoid of blacks, was that the people here shared the same views as him when it came to race. He thought he would've fit in just fine, but quickly he found out he was at the bottom of the social ladder. Still he fought for acceptance, hating to be denied by the same people he would kill and die for. He and majority of the people here did share the same views but over time, he figured out what differentiates him from everybody else—they were all Masons and Eastern Stars; everybody, from the male gardener and the female receptionist to the top male and female clients.

These people were bigger than discrimination and supremacy over others. They are the force behind racism. They were mayors, lawyers, politicians, police officers, doctors. He even ran into Judge Young, who questioned him about his mother's well-being. His coworkers, kids of clients, were mostly college students preparing to replace their parents or add on to their families' influence. He wondered what strings his mama pulled to place him in this atmosphere. Realizing he's the lone nutter and knowing Masonry could give him the influence he needed to start his own small militia of soldiers, he became determined to get in where he could. He made his intent known on several occasions; speaking to several different people he thought could help him.

Back inside the dining hall where everyone seemed to be busing themselves, Jillian guessed whoever was coming had to be someone of top importance. Everyone was on their peas and cues. The head manager, the highest ranking Mason working at the country club, was overseeing everything.

Being one to always put on his best performance whenever the spotlights were on, Jillian began to clean the dining room beyond the best of his ability. Inspecting his own work before he alerted his manager he was done, Jillian bumped into somewhat of an associate of his when she wasn't around everybody else and questioned his curiosity. "So what's all the hype about. Who are we expecting?"

Setting the silverware on each table, Melinda answered Jillian without looking at him. "This is supposed to be a Republican event hosted by Mr. Charlie Lynch."

"Charlie Lynch!" Jillian exclaimed, full of high spirit, remembering Job telling him about old man Mr. Charlie and surprised a real-life legend was coming here.

"Old man Mr. Charlie himself," she said, hearing how excited he was. Instantly she felt sorry for him. "You know Jillian, everything isn't for everybody. Maybe you should just go home." She kept her eyes on her task while she tried to hint to him what she wasn't supposed to.

"Take off and miss meeting a grand master dragon? I wouldn't miss this for nothing in the world."

He totally misunderstood her. Frustrated because she could be severely punished by doing what she was doing but for her like of him she tried again. "No Jillian," she kept her eyes averted, so it will be hard to tell she was talking to him. Continuing about her work, she said, "You should go. Quit this place. Get out of here."

"Quit!" Jillian repeated her words to him, still missing her true intentions and mistaking it for a form of degradation. He looked at her as if she was crazy and opened his mouth to give her a piece of his mind but she quickly turned and walked away from him.

She understood why certain things happen to certain people.

Fuming while he looked at her back, walking away from him, ironically he became a complete hypocrite. Jillian said to himself, "Everybody's got to be better than somebody!" forgetting he felt he was better than a whole race of people.

Deciding to go take himself a quick hidden break in the broken sauna room to clear his mind, Jillian sat in the sauna and sweated out his feelings, trying to find repose in himself. Being here reminded him of being in prison, trying to be accepted by the wrong people. Part of him wanted to say, "to hell with them," and the rest of him thought about the influential power he could have if he joined the Masonry.

As he was thinking hard on his best choice of action, audible voices in the sauna next to his broke his concentration. "Mr. Charlie, I don't see how we're going to get him to change his mind or better yet his views. He has the NAACP behind him, and slowly he's gathering all the African Americans in the Senate to advocate his issue. Surely, when it reaches the state, we'll have all the blacks in South Carolina arguing his case, causing an outcry for us to act. And if we fail to act, it will reach Washington and that will cause a nationwide outcry. Mr. Charlie, he knows this, which is why he's not backing off and why he's not taking the payoff. He's a servant of the good Lord Jesus Christ. It's against his religion, so he says. This guy is aiming to kill and he's going to. We have to stop him."

"I don't give a damn if he prayed to Allah seven times a day. I'm not about to allow some damn nigger pastor ruin so much over his fucking morals. He won't take the bribe?" Mr. Charlie asked, already knowing he won't.

"No, sir."

"Good! I got something he can't refuse to change everything about him. He's aiming to kill, well so am I."

Jillian listened on as they spoke about matters he had no understanding of. From what Job told him of Mr. Charlie, he only knew he was the highest-ranking member of the Aryan brotherhood in the state of South Carolina. But hearing him now, he knew Mr. Charlie was also into politics as well as Masonry. Feeling this may be his only chance to meet the legendary Mr. Charlie Lynch and the opportunity he needs to elevate up the social ladder, Jillian thought an intentional accidental bump into in the hallway of the sauna rooms would be perfect.

He checked his watch. It was 5:20 p.m. The event starts at six, so he knew they were going to be leaving the sauna at any moment. Jillian stepped out of the sauna to get into position to cross path with Mr. Charlie and heard someone call his name.

"Jillian."

Looking back at the young lady he was positive he'd never seen before, he asked. "And you are?"

"Someone you're interested in meeting," she said, seductively approaching him, "and someone you will never see again."

"How would you know that?" he asked skeptically.

She took her finger with her red nail, gestured him closer to her, and automatically he followed her. Jillian hated blacks but this mixed girl had a charm about her.

She gently brushed the side of his cheek, leaned forward, and whispered in his ear, "I know everything!" Nervously Jillian swallowed. "And I am the answer to all your problems. Not him." She gestured to Mr. Charlie who was coming out of the sauna with two other males.

"Princess Sadiasia," he greeted her with a peck on her hand as she acknowledged him back with a courteous slight bow of the head, then greeted the other two men with equal respect.

As always, he was overlooked. After they passed, Princess Sadiasa spoke to him with loving eyes. "I can get you what you want Jillian. Just come with me." She reached her hand out to him and saw him hesitate. "If you're smart like I know you are, I don't have to tell you this one decision will change your whole life. What you don't know is, you have been chosen. Chosen to serve."

He wanted to take the offer, but his intuition was stopping him. Something was off; he sensed it. He thought about Melinda's words, "I think I'll pass. I'm not sure if I belong here. You know everything isn't for everybody."

Smiling because she knew what he didn't, she told him. "That was really the wrong answer. The chosen are *choiceless*. Your future has already been decided. And you," she pointed to him, "just sealed it in a very bad way. Tsk, tsk." She sucked her teeth, shook her head in disappointment, then snapped her fingers.

"I decide my own future," Jillian managed to say before strong hands came out of nowhere and seized him. "Hey, what the heck. Get the fuck off me." He jerked in the man's grasped who latched on to him.

"Shhh!" she tried to quiet him. "When I'm done, you will only remember what I tell you," Princess Sadasia told him then turned to her henchman. "Take him." The massive henchman cocked back and struck Jillian in the dome of his head, knocking him unconscious.

Seven hours later, Princess Sadiasia walked into the room of Mr. Charlie, where he waited her return. "How did it go?" he asked.

"As expected. We shot him up with several drugs, ran test on him to see if he accepted the programing, and now you can say he is literally a walking zombie."

"Good, that's very good. Mr. Booth was a good decision. No traces, right?"

"Only one—his mother, but she won't be around too long. The press will play this off as another white kid gone crazy. We've planted the perfect smoke screen. The masses won't be able to see through it. Add this to the recent events going on in South Carolina and around America, and we will have the country advocating our wants. The enforcement of gun laws which will further our agenda of disarming the population, preventing them from defending themselves under martial law; and when Armageddon begins, you will get your bill passed," Princess Sadiasia said the last part with little significance. "I say it's a win-win situation."

Taking a sip of his liquor, Mr. Charlie said, "We're devils."

"No, we're Gods. Creating us a Garden of Eden while everybody else be damned to the pits of eternal fire."

CHAPTER 16

"I would like everyone to turn in their Bibles to," he drew out the word *to*, "the book of Job, chapters 1 and 2," Pastor Emanuel said to the thirteen people attending Wednesday night Bible study class at Graham AME Baptist Church. "Son, would you like a Bible to read along?" he asked the stranger who joined them today.

Tight lipped, Jillian said, "I just came to listen," as he sat in a pew behind an elderly woman.

"Amen brother." The pastor said.

Jillian thought to himself, *I'm not your brother.*

"As long as you get the word in you, that's all that matters. Sister Anna Mae will surely allow you to look on if you choose to."

Sister Anna Mae turned in her seat to reassure the stranger behind her that he could look on along with her if he changed his mind. Upon making eye contact with the mushroom haircut, young Caucasian male and seeing the red veins lining the whites of his eyes, stopping at his laser-blue pupils, smelling the malice reeking from his pores and feeling his devilishness vibrating through the air, she forgot her reason for facing him.

Her heart told her this young man was troubled badly.

She wanted to remove him from their services, but her intuition was in conflict with her intellect. God's good word, "Thou shall not judge" taught her to trust in God and not herself. So she followed her mind and not her heart.

Remembering her purpose, she nodded to the young man who stared hard back at her and turned back in her seat trying to shake the devil out of her heart.

"Now I would like for someone to read chapter 1, verses 6 to 12." An adolescent female who came to Bible study along with her mother, began to read the scripture. When she was done, the pastor said, "All right thank you, young Ms. Ashley. Now what's going on here is, Satan came to the Lord along with the sons of god and the Lord asks him, 'Where does he come from?' Satan tells the Lord he was 'wandering the earth.' Now the Lord knows what Satan is up to, he's looking for someone he can turn into his ranks, someone he can manipulate from one side to another. So the Lord set Job, his servant, before him and tells Satan, 'There is none like him on the earth. One who fears god and shuns evil,' enticing Satan with one of his worthiest servants. Satan goes on to tell the Lord why Job is worthy to him. 'If you take away all you have given him, surely Job will curse you.' Testing the loyalty of his servant, the Lord gives all Job has to Satan, with one exception, 'don't touch him.' See congregation, temptation is a two-way street. Not only is Job being tempted by the Lord but also by Satan. Temptation can help you and it can hinder you."

"Amen." Another brother attending Bible study stood up and shouted to what the preacher was saying.

"But it's up to Job, to us, to overcome Satan's temptation and live for God." The pastor preached on as Jillian heard another voice in his mind, the voice of God. He pulled out his seventeen-shot .45 caliber and sat it on the pew beside him.

Sister Anna Mae sat there with the book open in her lap, too uncomfortable to get into the word. During the whole service, she has been fighting the urge to confront the young man behind her. *Maybe he was on drugs*, she thought, *and needed this*. She rationalized then heard a distinctive click coming from something metal directly behind her. "Lord, please don't let that be what I think it is," she silently prayed before she turned around. "Young man, are you alright?"

Jillian grinned then upped his pistol. *Blaw!* The gunshot sounded off in the hollows of the church. The close range shot blew her face off, sending her brains into the open Bible. Screams erupted and some were stunned to silence. The brother who was already on his feet, felt as if God was on his side and charged toward Jillian. Three rapid shots stopped the false force inside of him and splattered blood all over the preacher. "Don't fucking move," Jillian demanded waving the gun around, halting everybody's chance for an escape.

"Put the gun down, brother," the preacher said, confronting Jillian as he stood in the middle of the aisle. With both hands up in the air, the pastor said, "Please," right before a single round from the massive caliber weapon went off and entered his neck causing blood to squirt out his wound and mouth. "Kill the pastor," the voice in his head repeated over and over so Jillian aimed his second shot to the pastor's head. *Blaw!* Killing him before his body slumped to the ground.

Jillian turned to find three people trying to escape and in rapid fire he sent a volley of shots in their direction, stopping them inches away from the exit.

Following the holy voice in his head, "Then kill all the witnesses." Jillian did as told and sorted out the others hidden under the pews throughout the church and gave them all a shot in the head.

Finding Ashley and her mother hidden in the choir stand, hugging each other, Jillian lifted his gun, right before the mother asked, "Why are you doing this?" and pulled the trigger. *Click click*! God told him the gun might do this and if it did, then what to do. He said, "God sent me here to kill all black people."

Detective Zori stood in the middle of the tragedy. Inside Graham AME Baptist Church, eleven innocent victims lay dead, covered with white sheets. *A fucking church!* he thought to himself, figuring profanity wouldn't matter in the wake of a gunman killing eleven innocent people in God's house.

Forensics were everywhere, skimming the place clean for any and every piece of evidence they could find. Outside, firetrucks lined the streets, along with ambulances that were taking care of the two survivors who both gave details of the crime and the suspect.

Being the lead detective on the case, Detective Zori knew he had his work cut out for him and it didn't make it any better that the alphabet boys, the FEDs, were popping up already. Last week, it was nine firefighters who lost their lives trying to stop a building from burning. Today, it's eleven Bible study-goers. What is America coming to? The Bible predicted these days were coming, when the world would be at war with other countries, as well as inside their own. Poverty, famine, and diseases would be at an all-time high. Killings going on inside schools, movies and now churches. Saying a silent prayer for his kids and their kids to come, Detective Zori felt like nowhere was safe.

"Sir." His assistant detective came rushing toward him. "I did what you told me to do and it was a hit. The street cameras got him twice. One exiting the building getting into his truck and the one worth the pot of gold, the traffic light caught his plates. Truck registered to a Jillian Booth." The assistant handed him a photograph of the suspect leaving the church and Jillian's mugshot. "They are one and the same. We got our guy!"

"Address?" Detective Zori asked anxiously and ready to bust this kid.

"Lexington, South Carolina, about two hours from here."

"He drives two hours from home to shoot up a church," Detective Zori said more to himself, trying to process the weirdness of him passing two hundred other churches and coming here. "Call Lexington PD. Alert them to what's happening here. This is a very sensitive situation. Suspect is armed, dangerous and inside their county. It's a long shot he'll be home, but if he is, don't fuck up."

"Yes, sir!"

"Jillian!" his mother called out to him from the other side of his room door. "Are you okay in there?" Jillian was unresponsive like he's been since he came home pushing through her front door, looking half crazy, running to his room. She got no response. "I know you can hear me Jill Jill. I hope you're not messing around with that stuff again." She sniffed the door seeing if she could smell anything through his door crack. "Jillian?" she called out to him again, angry he was ignoring her. "Well fine damn it. I'll just go to the store myself and I am not getting you anything since you want to ignore me." Taking a step to walk off, she stopped and said, "Don't burn down my house, Jillian." She then went on her way downstairs. She grabbed her phone and keys and walked out the front door at the same time a strike team was in full-combat gear was about to enter her house.

"May I help you?" she asked, frozen in her step upon seeing men with black masks on her porch.

"I advise you to get on the ground and remain quiet," the lead officer said with his gun on her face.

Breaking News

"The gunman who left eleven dead and two alive to tell their story has been apprehended by Lexington PD, with the help of Charleston's PD in what seems to be an interdepartmental operation. Details of the operation later, but now here is a clip from an interview of Charleston's chief of police.

"Thanks to our street cameras and surviving victims, we were able to get a lead and identification of the suspect which ultimately led to his arrest. Thanks to the whole Lexington Police Department for stepping up to the plate and lending us a helping hand in a time of need which allowed us to capture someone who has not only done our city an act of injustice but our country as well. My heart, prayers, and condolences go out to each and every family member of every victim in this insensible crime. I'm glad we're able to bring justice to this perp and not allowed him to slip through our fingers. Last but not least, I would like to thank God."

"That was the chief of Charleston's Police Department on this tragic day, eleven lives had been lost at Graham AME Church. Reports found that this may have been a crime of hate. The suspect posted pictures of himself on Facebook along with the murder weapon in the background and a Confederate flag minutes before the crime took place. More on the details of the intradepartmental operation when we return. I'm Brittany Johnson Channel 10 News."

Columbia, South Carolina

"Take the flag down! Take the flag down!" Hundreds of protesters stood outside of South Carolina's State House in Columbia, with banners and posters practicing their First Amendment, the freedom of speech and the right to protest.

The flag symbolizes racial division; and too many lives, black and white, have been lost in its name. The protesters believed it was a disgrace for it to fly in the sky of their state. Also for someone to commit the heinous act of murdering eleven innocent black people in a place of worship after supporting and promoting this flag on Facebook the day before, is further confirmation of the inequality the flag represents. Protesters wanted justice and equality as they chanted, "We want justice, we want equality, take it down!"

Inside the State House, a man very few knew but held more power than the governor made a phone call while looking out the window to where protesters gathered. "Why in the hell would you cause an uproar about such a thing?" he said vehemently when the he heard his conspirator, the granddaughter of the most powerful family in South Carolina, answered her phone.

"We needed a tangible reason and what better way than what the South was built on, racism!"

"You could've blame it on anything."

"And the real reason could have been exposed. You wouldn't want it to be known you wanted the honorable senator slash pastor dead because he was threatening your livelihood, now would you? The truth is only one thought away. And please keep one thing in mind, I am mixed." Princess Sadasia chuckled to herself.

"My family orchestrated that war. I fly that flag as a remembrance in my state. Now with this heat, it'll have to be taken down."

"There're losses and gains in this war, Mr. Charlie. You may have lost your flag, but you gain undisputable dominion. You got that and your flag will always fly in your heart and the hearts of your people."

"Oh my gosh!"

"Is everything alright?"

"The black bitch is climbing the poll. I've got to go." Mr. Charlie hung up on the princess and called his guard. "I want that black cunt bitch arrested immediately." He pointed out the window to the woman removing the Confederate flag from the state poll. "And fly my damn flag."

Outside, the protesters cheered as their fellow advocate removed the flag and threw it to the ground where they burned it where it felled.

"Light that damn thing Andy and let's be through with this place before the niggers crawl out their graves and attack us." Billy, a Klan's member dressed in his white robe, told his brother who was adding the final touches to their mischief.

"Hold on just a minute. Let me get this thing here good and gassed before I spark it. Give these niggers a rude awakening. This is still the South," Andy said, tossing gasoline to their makeshift cross. "See Billy we go quiet and they start talking, but this here will give them something to talk about. Come on, let's pull it up and tie it down." Together they pulled the rope, lifting the cross up and staked it into the ground. "Here Billy Boy. The honors all yours." Andy handed Billy a lit cigarette. Billy took it, inhaled a drag of it and tossed the cigarette at their handy work, brightening up the early morning sky.

Since the Mt. Grahmn A.M.E shooting, racial conflict was on a major all-time rise all over America and especially in South Carolina. Badge-on-black violence was rising; both blacks and whites were being lynched. The Klan was marching again. Random robberies of everyday white citizens were rising in predominately black areas. America was in straight chaos.

Pulling up to her church for early Sunday services, Pastor Carter was surprised to see fire trucks at her establishment, putting out what seemed to be a burning cross. Gasping, not believing someone would do such a thing nowadays, tears began to stream from her eyes. A couple days ago, someone shot through a church's window on James Island, hurting no one. Before that, someone killed eleven innocent people in another church. The wickedness of the world was becoming too grave and great. Ignorance was at an all-time high.

Hopping out of her car, her deacon, a white man named David, approached her and hugged her tightly. "If there was ever a time for Jesus to return, now will be a good time," she told him through tears.

CHAPTER 17

"I got my keys, water bottle, TV's off, the stove's off. Let's go!" Chris said to himself, making sure he didn't leave anything behind or on as he felt himself and looked around. Feeling alive and hopeful, with his new mind-set, he made his way to the front door.

The phone rang.

"Why not?" he asked then turned around to answer it. "Hello?"

"Wasup pal. How are you feeling?" A friend of his past life, Gary, called to check on him.

"Just fine!" Chris told him. He has been preparing for this phone call since he decided to turn his life around.

"I'm glad to hear that pal. Listen here buddy, we're marching today and you should come join us. It's been a long time since we had Baby Cooper in line with us boys. How's your brother doing?"

"Actually, I haven't spoken to him in a while." Chris told him. But truthfully, he hasn't been accepting any of his calls. He spoke to Tommy once and realized his situation didn't spark a small light inside him, that maybe he was wrong. So Chris felt distance between them was best. In fact, he distanced his entire new self, from every possible encounter of his old self. "Gary I'll have to pass on your offer. You know," Chris started trying to recall exactly what and how he was going to distance himself from his closest way of life, "losing my wife and daughter, my brother. I decided to do things differently. I thank you for calling and checking up on me."

Gary blurted in. "Sure sure, Chris. I understand completely. What you went through was a mighty lot for one man to carry. Things like that take time to heal. You just hang in there pal, stay strong. You just give me a call whenever you're ready to come on around. We'll be here for you."

"Yeah thanks, but I don't think that'll be happening. Hello?" Chris said into the receiver. "Hello?" his words fell on unheard ears. Gary had already hung up.

Chris hung up as well and took in a deep breath, wishing that was the end of that chapter in his life, but knew it wasn't. He headed out the house while double checking himself and the house for the last time.

Cranking up his car, Chris spotted his flag flying above his front door and thought about it, then hopped back out. He took it down, looked at it, relishing all this way of life took from him, heard the trash truck coming and tossed it inside the garbage can by the road. *Like Tom, Gary will get the message*, he thought and hopped back into his car and pulled off.

"Changing your life isn't that hard if you really wanted to do it!" Camilla realized this in the three months she spent living with Kellyn and getting her life together.

The first two weeks were the hardest. She dubbed that period her system *cleaning*. Her body rejected any and everything she tried to put into it while at the same time pushed all and everything she had inside her out through her mouth or her ass. She was literally withdrawing.

Happy to be alive, she came upon her healing process and with the help of Kellyn and the gift from God and strong will, she has gotten a job, has remained drug-free since that fatal day and was on her way to her new three-bedroom apartment after coming back from a group home, seeing Rayquan and Richie, who she was fighting the only baby daddy, the government, she ever knew for. "Kellyn, my babies were so happy to see me. I never saw them look at me the way they did today girl! Never!" Camilla told Kellyn, who was taking her downtown to look at her new apartment with elation in her voice. Seeing Kellyn smile at her accomplishments, Camilla had to thank her for she played a major role in her success.

"Milla girl please. All I did was help you do you."

"And for that, I thank you. Some people need that strong person to help push them forward in life. I couldn't have done this without you."

"Will since that's the case, you're welcome Milla and for your information, you look damn good. If you were my mama, I'll be happy to see you looking like Beyonce too girl."

Looking at herself in the mirror, Camilla asked. "I look good girl?" Loving the sound of those words being said to her.

"Better than Beyonce!"

"You such an angel." Camilla continued to admire herself in the mirror.

Riding downtown at Meeting Street, they rode into a huge mass of people crowded in the streets with signs and shirts that said, "Black lives matter!"

"Girl what's going on here?" Camilla asked.

"It looks like they're protesting." Kellyn was amazed by all the people. "Look at all these people, they're everywhere." She couldn't drive forward another inch. A police officer gestured for her to turn.

"The Charleston's eleven incident," Camilla said sadly because she knew family members of the victims.

"I don't think our two voices should go unheard. Want to go park and join the voice?" Kellyn asked, thinking about Trimpell.

"Where are we parking?"

After parking on one of the side streets, Kellyn and Camilla joined the protest. Someone was speaking into a microphone that blasted through speakers. Tapping a young lady on the arm, Kellyn asked, "Who is that speaking?"

The young lady said, "Some guy name Fella and he is strong!" She said referring to his speech then she looked at Camilla who was digging into her purse, and asked having the feeling she had seen her somewhere before. "Do I know you?"

"No sweetheart, you don't actually know me but you have seen me before." Handing her a five-dollar bill Camilla said, "You helped me get where I am today and I told you, whenever I saw you again, I was going to repay you. Thank you!"

"Oh my god, you're the lady from the pantry that one night. You look totally different look at you!" The young lady said surprisingly.

Glancing over to Kellyn, Camilla smiled again then told the young lady. "You played a big part in this. You and Ms. Lisa."

"Awww!" The young lady hugged Camilla.

"Mahogany right?" Camilla remembered her name from the name tag she was wearing. When the young lady acknowledged that was her name Camilla said, "Let's hear what this Fella guy has to say."

"Unity people, that's the key. Unity. We must unite amongst each other and stop the separation, racial division, and hate toward one another. And not just over our skin color but over every jealousy, envy, over every evil that's rooted in our hearts. See we are who make up the world, the people, and if we are not right then the world isn't right because we are the world. If we can change ourselves then we can change the world. This goes for every system, the judicial, the religious, the government. We are the people that fill those positions. You want to see a change in the police system, then change yourself and that's gone change your kids and when their kids get older and become our next generation of law enforcement, they won't be out here dragging middle-school girls on their backs out of classrooms for disrespect or shooting little nine-year-old boys for looking like suspects or killing high school kids for looking threatening, planting Tasers on black men just to have a reason to murder them. See, these are the tragedies that will be avoided by changing our hearts today for our future in tomorrow. No, we won't see a change in the world overnight, but as long as we strive and fight for this change, it's going to happen.

"I was listening to Steve Harvey's morning show this morning, and he said, 'We can desire something but don't have the discipline to go after what we desire.' See we may want reform, we may want change but don't want to do, don't want to fight for what it takes to reform or change. Therefore, we don't really desire what we think and tell ourselves we desire. We want what we want, but want is not a strong enough desire to change. We have to discipline ourselves to change. I just didn't pick up a pen and started writing to you. No! I laid in bunk and thought about what I was going to write till I fell asleep, then I woke up and I wrote till my hand cramped. Got discouraged many times but I kept on writing and now here I am, speaking to you. I fought for this and we are going to have to do the same if we want to change anything about ourselves, about the world. If you don't believe me, ask Cam Newton, Lebron James, Floyd Mayweather, Barack Obama. Or better yet, asked that woman in the crowd standing next to you how hard she fought to give up drugs or ask that man how hard it was for him to give up his hate. Oftentimes, it takes something drastic to happen—a financial plummet, death of a loved one, and so forth—to happen in our lives before we start to desire change. That's so sad but it's so true. For me, it was ten years in prison, then nine months later, another five more months for me to really desire a change. I stand before you today, apologetically that it took the lives of Trayvon Martin, Michael Brown, Zavion Dobson, Freddie Gray, Sandra Bland, nine lives in Emanuel AME and the millions of other lives lost for me to write this and speak my peace. For that, I apologize. This message needed to be heard. I just ask one thing of you all today: 'Let this be an eye opener, your desire to change.' We don't need another civil war, more separation, more hate, more racism, more murder. We need more peace, more unity, more love, and more life. We need to forever love life and all things in existence. That's Fella."

"The Klans here!" someone yelled breaking the silence of the crowd as the Klan marched up to the protest.

Suddenly the sound of the crowd grew as everyone looked around for men in white robes.

Being at the back of the crowd, Kellyn and Camilla were directly across the street from the Klansmen who stood in single-file line formation, facing them with Confederate flags flying on small poles and wild dogs barking aggressively on leashes held in their hands. Both ladies were scared to death, not knowing what the future held in the seconds to come. Grabbing ahold of each other's hands and clenching their grasp tightly, so they wouldn't get separated by the mass of people, a single Klansman stepped forward.

"Everybody just remain calm. This is a peaceful protest." Fella tried to calm everyone down.

It seemed the second civil war was on the verge of popping off. The riot squad came and separated the face-off by lining up in the middle of the street. On one side of the road was a huge crowd of mixed protesters and on the other side was the Klan with a growing number of supporters joining them by the second.

"Excuse me, excuse me." Chris came and parted the crowd, making his way to where the Klan was. He was ready to show his face and now was the perfect time. He saw who he knew to be Gary in the middle of the street dressed in his all-black robe. He walked over to face him. "Excuse me!" he told Kellyn and Camilla and stood in front of them. He caught Gary's attention.

"Looks like you're on the wrong side of the street there, pal?"

"Actually Gary, I'm on the right side of the street. If my wife and child were here, this is the side of the street they would want to be on, with the people, not against them."

"You're making a very bad decision here, boy. That side of the street is the one who took your family from you."

"No! Hate took my family from me. Being on the wrong side of the street took my family from me, my brother from me. You need to open your eyes Gary. It's a new day in time. People are moving forward, coming together as one while you're still holding on to a thing of the past. Look at you all—only cowards hide behind masks."

Kellyn and Camilla stepped up beside Chris hearing him standing up against the Klan and they each took ahold of one of his hands. The crowd of people standing behind them stepped up and grabbed ahold of each other's hands. Chris looked at them both and felt the power of unity in his palms.

"Chris, you're making a fool of yourself, of your family. Your great ancestors helped started this. You belong over here with us, with your own kind. Don't do this to yourself."

Chris smiled. "You've never been where I've been, Gary, so I don't expect you to understand but I will tell you this. Sometimes to love yourself, you have to lose all you love. Then once you hit the bottom, there's only one way to go and that's up. If this," he lifted his hands with Kellyn's and Camilla's in his as the crowd behind him did the same, "is wrong. Loving one another, coming together as one, is wrong. Then I'm sorry Gary. But I don't want to be right."

THE END